# THEY THE F...

## Court High Book 1

## By Eden O'Neill

**THEY THE PRETTY STARS:** Court High Book 1

Copyright © 2020 by Eden O'Neill

**Cover Design** by Veronica Eden

# Table of Contents

1

The air tasted stale here, tasted cold. It wasn't like California. It wasn't like home. Contrary to popular belief, my name being December didn't automatically adjust me to the colder-than-balls Midwestern chill.

*I'm going to die when fucking winter hits.*

I groaned, seriously questioning my sister's sanity. She'd somehow managed to live here most of her whole life.

*You need to get up.*

I closed my eyes instead, delaying the enviable and my father, who no doubt was moving around downstairs. I hadn't heard the door click shut yet, my room directly above.

*You need to get up. Get up, Em.*

My sister's voice haunted as I pulled myself from warm sheets. They'd been the words she said to me when she left me, left me to move halfway across the country to live with our dad. She left with him after our mom passed, cancer a son of a bitch. I stayed in Cali because that's where we all had lived, our aunt taking me in to live with her. I'd been eight and Paige had been nine, and I didn't need any more damn changes in my life at the time, which had been the reason I stayed. Paige hadn't, though, and it'd been the first time she left me.

This last summer was the second.

I dragged my head up, working my shoulders in an attempt to work the kinks out from an unfamiliar bed. Dad had given me the pick of the house, but I still hadn't gotten used to the sleeping situation yet. With a lazy reach, I grabbed my phone, pressing a button to check for texts. As predicted, Aunt Celeste had checked in on me.

**Aunt Celeste:** Just wanted to wish you luck on your first day. Let me know if you hear any changes about your sister, but I don't want you to get your hopes up.

As I heard all this before I left, I simply texted back, *I'll be cool and thanks. I will.*

After doing a quick scan of my social media accounts, I stood to hard and creaking floorboards. Aunt Celeste's and my place never creaked, never any give on cheap tiles and dingy carpet. It always worked for us, and lights always stayed on, my stomach fed. Bearing cold creaks with naked feet, I stretched and moved into the bathroom.

*Yeah, I have my own bathroom… never getting used to that.*

I checked more social media inside, then peeled myself away long enough to get washed up for my first day at a new school in the middle of a term. I supposed that decision had ultimately been mine, but not made because I actually wanted to uproot myself

2

from my aunt, my friends, and everything I loved about my life. If I had things my way, I'd be back in LA on a bus to *my own* school with a Pop-Tart in my hand.

*Paige saw fit to ruin all that.*

My older sister better be okay because, if she wasn't, I wouldn't be—this I knew and the reason I made myself put some clothes on and trek downstairs in a house familiar to her and not to me. When Dad had been offered a job that took him *almost* as far away as he could possibly get from our old lives and Paige chose to live with him, I'd been pretty damn shattered for a long time. Paige and I had been more than sisters. We were friends, so yeah, I'd been hella hurt. In the end, I'd been a big girl and eventually gotten over it. There were more opportunities for her with our dad and I got that. She got stuff here with Dad, cars and fancy schools like the one I got to go to today.

"You miss your uniform or something?"

It also got her dad, Dad's eye, and consequently, his scrutiny. I'd naively hoped he'd take his breakfast in the actual nook designated for that. He had all week since I arrived.

My presence known, I eased into the kitchen, my dad taking inventory of my acid-washed jean shorts and oversize top. He snapped his paper over the breakfast bar. "I had Rosanna leave it out for you."

The academy uniform I missed, but probably because she'd placed it in my closet and not out in the open. Rosanna was his housekeeper, and I'd been told if I needed anything to go to her—anything to avoid actually dealing with me.

I wet my lips. "She probably put it in the closet or something. I'll change after breakfast."

His look was dismissive, the same eyes I had with their deep brown and far less passion for life than he had when he'd been with Mom. My dad had always been a bit of a hard-ass, but when Mom passed, the switch went into overdrive. He didn't deal with any type of emotions. He just worked, all that easier than other things. When Mom died, it gave him an excuse to fall into the rich and opulent life he'd traded for, basically, my hippy mom. She'd been into herbs and crystals where he'd been into stocks and the sports section. Those stocks and his background in banking got him this big-ass house and a fancy job that allowed him to wear those suits he wore at the breakfast table. Most would say I probably took my looks from my dad, straight dark hair, long nose with a button tip, and curved chin. I got my hips from my mom, though, and poor Paige, she'd gotten the crap end of the stick when it came to that. She was nearly as flat-chested as our dad, but she had been skinny, though. So I guess she got that.

Trying to keep the interactions with my dad quick, I headed toward the pantry to get the Pop-Tarts I brought over with me.

"Don't bother with those," he said right as I touched the box. "I'm having Rosanna toss them all out. You don't need all that sugary crap."

My jaw working, I got off my tiptoes and returned my feet to the floor. "What am I supposed to eat?"

"I had Rosanna make you a green smoothie and some eggs. You live with me, you're going to do some changes."

My peripheral caught the foreign drink on the counter, green and no doubt filled with things that'd make me gag this morning. The thing that definitely would make me gag was next to them, though: the eggs under the glass dome filled with steam.

I gripped the counter, turning. "I told you I'm a vegan, Dad. Have been for three years." As he tended to listen to every other word, I supposed he missed that.

He moved the paper. "You mean to tell me Pop-Tarts are vegan?"

"Those kind are, yeah."

"Well, you're not eating them, and I thought vegans were supposed to be healthy. I swear to God, you and your sister and these alternative lifestyles."

By "alternative lifestyle," he meant my sister's sexuality, something he clearly still hadn't dealt with and my sister came out in middle school. Dad was old school amongst other things and always, *always* sought for perfection. That perfection had been my sister's downfall, and I was sure the reason she left. Dad directed a finger. "Drink the smoothie. You'll be all right until lunch."

I supposed, if he had it his way, I wouldn't eat at all, just so he wouldn't have to know about my existence. I'd been acting as his little dark cloud on the West Coast for years now, his secret daughter he hadn't had to deal with. Maybe if he had, I wouldn't have had to be a secret.

And Paige wouldn't have really left to protect me from his wrath.

This conversation clearly over, I went to the kitchen pegboard for keys. I'd been given full use of the cars there, which I was taking full advantage of once I changed and could get the hell out of this house.

"You won't need those for school." Dad got the jump on me again, folding his paper crisply before standing. "Hubert will take you to school. He's warming the car now for you."

Hubert was his driver. "How will you get to work?"

"I'm taking the Rolls-Royce," he said, grabbing the driving clothes I hadn't noticed by his own kitchen plate. My dad would have a driver and not even use it. Back before Mom died, he hadn't quite reached the level of success he had now, something he never failed to wave in front of my aunt's face whenever he saw her. She had to work sixty-hour weeks as a nurse to put food on the table. He merely had to make a phone call with a few clients. He grabbed his briefcase. "Have a good day at school and be mindful of your curfew. Things won't be like they were back with your aunt. I have rules here."

He did have rules, didn't he? And what happened to me in LA had nothing to do with my aunt, or where I lived. I was sure he'd never see it that way, so there wasn't a point in defending myself or my geography. My dad had placed me in a tight little box, and as far as he was concerned, that's where I would stay. Also, something told me his sentiment of me "having a good day" was more for formality than anything. I didn't believe he actually cared to wish me well. I was an obligation, his daughter, and he had to say things like that.

He started to walk off but stopped. "Let me know if you hear anything about your sister. You know, kids talking or whatever?"

Yes, I'd definitely tell the one person what he wanted to know about the very reason I stood in this house instead of on the way to my own school. Paige not being here now had everything to do with him and absolutely nothing to do with me.

Dad's lips turned down. "Though, don't you get your hopes up. She's probably dicking around like she always tends to do. She'll make her way back when she feels like it. Have fun waiting around while she gets her shit together."

I'd blanch if this wasn't expected, my sister "dicking around" to the point where even my aunt wasn't concerned anymore. Paige and my dad got into things so much that her just up and leaving had become old hat for years since she came to live with him. It wasn't unheard of for me to wake up with my sister on my aunt's couch or even sleeping in my desk chair after she took a red-eye to get away from him. It also wasn't unheard of for her just to leave town and ghost for days on end after she and Dad truly let into each other. She just needed space sometimes but she always popped up...

She'd never been gone an entire summer, though.

2

The school uniform rode up my ass like a son of a bitch, a literal atomic wedgie which I endured the entirety of the trip inside a chauffeured car. Maywood Heights was a smaller city, but not a sleepy town by any means. People were alive and well, maple leaves of gold and umber tones being raked up in yards the size of football fields. What I'd dubbed as McMansions followed one after the other, a far cry from the graffiti apartment complexes and litter-filled streets I came from. I didn't live exactly in the city, a suburb, and people didn't care about their shit like they did here. I had a feeling they might have given awards out for some of this landscaping.

*Jesus.*

Paige never talked about where she lived much during her visits. Sure, she talked about the basic shit, who she was sleeping with or the crap that went down with her and Dad, but the actual town, not so much. Crossing my legs, I attempted to adjust my skirt again, bracing myself for the day to come. When Paige moved away, we'd been in different grades. I mean, she was a year older than me at nineteen, but her tendencies to miss classes and I guess "dick around," as my dad would say, placed us both as seniors this year. At least, she would have been if she were here. The school had been told about this from what I understood. Though, my dad tended to keep his dirty laundry on the DL. As far as they knew, Paige simply wouldn't be attending school for the time being and his other daughter, me, would be finishing out her senior year here instead.

"Windsor Preparatory Academy, Ms. Lindquist. Would you like me to pull up right to the doors or is the start of the quad to your liking?"

Passing through gates with a crest comprised of orange and navy sections, another football field presented itself in the form of the quad. These people had a quad, many other chauffeured cars such as mine dropping off students with navy and sun-kissed ties, as well as pleated skirts that rode just as mine. These girls seemed to be used to it, though, the tights. Rosanna actually laid out knee-highs for my ass, but I wasn't having that. Putting up with nylons, I adjusted those, directing Hubert to take me to the main doors. The other kids seemed to get out early to meet each other for a longer walk, and hiding like a little bitch gave me time to gawk at them a little behind tinted glass.

*What have I gotten myself into?*

My plan was simple, be here and make myself known until my sister rescued me. She had a tendency of doing that, playing savior whenever I needed her. There's a reason she'd been so quick to leave with Dad, take the brunt of his parenting and keep the focus off me, and I wasn't unaware of the sacrifice she'd made all those years ago. Her dealing with our strict and sometimes cold father meant I never had to. She'd been there for me by ironically leaving me, so if I came here and word ultimately got back to her about it, she would be back.

She always showed up for me.

Hubert stopped in front of the large oak doors, and after handing me a bag filled with books, he directed me to see the headmaster first. There, I'd be told my schedule and instructed where to go. Basically, the baby bird would be thrown right out of the nest and into the prestigious halls of Windsor Prep.

"Your father instructed me to give you this card as well," he stated, handing me plastic over the seat. Black and heavy, the credit card already had my name on it. Hubert formed a smile behind a gray mustache. "For your lunches."

And I'd be sure to load it up with lots of Pop-Tarts and sugary crap. Just because he didn't want it in his house didn't mean I couldn't keep a few boxes in my locker.

"Thanks, Hubert. And for the ride."

"Of course. I'll be here when you get out. Two thirty on the dot."

I nearly made the man promise this, to save me from this place and what used to seem like a smart decision. Frankly, my sister would kill me if she knew I was at her school living with Dad. She really did always try to keep her life with Dad as separate as she could from me. I'd never been to visit her. She always came to me before I could, holidays and everything. When I did see my dad, it was because he came along for the ride. We really were the epitome of a "happy" family.

Gripping my bag, I scaled brick steps that matched the buildings situated in various sections of the quad. Students ventured to all facets of the place, but I'd been told the main building positioned at the center was where I needed to be. The fact that I didn't have to bypass security and metal detectors floored me upon entry of a building that smelled uniquely rife with age and upper class, and following the signs, I easily found the headmaster's office.

I think the large gorilla head had something to do with that.

I'd read the school's mascot was "The King" in the pamphlets Dad gave me to prepare, but seeing the motherfucker straight on was a sight. It bared sharp white fangs like actual King Kong, a mock growl at anything that dared to pass its bust. The headmaster had it on a column before his office, and I was sure the life-size version dancing on the football field in a felt costume did exactly what these people hoped it would to anyone going against them in a game. It was truly terrifying, giving me chills as I shook my head and passed. Inside, I was told to take a seat, and eventually, the school's headmaster, Principal Hastings, did see me. It took a sec. Apparently, he'd been in meetings most of the morning according to his secretary. By the time he saw me, I'd been more than ready to get this show on the road, shaking his hand and letting him welcome me into the institution. It was the traditional song and dance of a new student coming to a foreign school, but I'd honestly been surprised the person at the top of this place had to do something so arbitrary. I supposed the alumni dollars may have required it, so I sat for the introductions and, later, the handoff of my schedule. It was nothing fancy considering the grades I brought in here, and I was sure Dad had to make a couple phone calls just to get me into the place. I didn't consider myself dumb by any means but I was sure the public school curriculum was leagues behind the place that sported King Kong as its mascot.

"We're happy to have you here," Principal Hastings concluded with, placing his hands together on a wide oak desk. "Though, we were very sad to see Paige won't be joining us this year. Have you heard anything different about her?"

A town this size and school this elite, I wasn't surprised he'd heard about my sister going AWOL. He was probably one of many I'd hear either asking or whispering about her whereabouts in the days to come.

I opened my hands. "Your guess is as good as mine." Besides a few texts here and there at the beginning of the summer, I'd heard nothing from my sister, absolutely nothing, and I seemed to be the only one who worried about that. My sister may have had bouts of acting out, but never had she gone such an extended amount of time without word. Especially when it came to me. I shrugged. "I'm hoping with me being here she may come back."

This really was the plan. Places like this talked, people busybodies. She'd hear I was around.

At least I hoped.

Principal Hastings said nothing to that, simply nodding when he stood. "I hope you're right and she really will be missed around here in her absence. You'll be sure to let us know if you hear any changes?"

I told him I would, and after a quick shake, our meeting concluded with him escorting me out of his office. I was told I'd have a guide coming for me to take me to class, and he waited with me for a moment before excusing himself.

"I'm afraid I have another meeting, but you should be all right?"

I nodded as I would, but before he darted off, he waved a finger by his nose.

"This will have to be removed before you start your day, I'm afraid," he stated, referring to my nose ring. "We do have a strict dress code here, yes?"

I'd popped the hoop in outside of the scrutiny of my dad and in the privacy of a chauffeured car. Apologizing for the error, I removed it, and Principal Hastings left me to wait for my guide standing next to the scarier-than-shit simian bust. The King was giving me the eye like nothing else, and the urge to smoke hit me like a freight train.

*Shit.*

I usually only did weed when I was stressed and I was damn stressed. I figured I'd at least wait until lunch and bop off somewhere, but this guide was taking too long and I needed a smoke. After a quick scan of the halls, I decided to take the map Principal Hastings gave me along with my class schedule and find some place to hide and light a joint. My travels took me outside, and it was like God was looking down on me because the bell signaling the end of class sounded and the sudden crowds allowed me to blend in. Eventually, I peeled off from the packs of students and escaped behind the administrative offices. The back of campus had an outlook of the water, a little lake of some kind, and venturing, I noticed a moderately sized shack. Considering everyone else was headed in the opposite direction, I darted inside the shack and internally screamed sweet relief to find myself alone.

The place was a boathouse. I mean, stacks upon stacks of what appeared to be long canoes were stored on elevated shelving and I touched one. Obviously, this school had some kind of rowing team as well, and I took advantage of the fact when I decided to light up my joint amongst the clusters of boats.

*Damn, did I need this.*

I allowed the drug to filter through me as I took a seat in a boat aisle. Using my backpack as a pillow, I lay on it, crossing my ankles and watched as my smoke drifted, then clouded toward the top of the house.

I closed my eyes, feeling the release of the drug before a rustle behind nearly made me drop the joint.

*Shit.*

I started to put it out but stopped at the sound of a little whimper. Getting on my knees, I followed that sound to another aisle and alarm hit me at the sight of a pair of little eyes underneath a boat. I lowered, and when those eyes turned out to be puppy dog eyes surrounded by dark chocolate fur, alarm instantly shifted to warmth. A puppy, a real live puppy, was under there, and getting closer, I made out the breed, a dark Labrador. I had a friend who had one once, and I recognized it easily.

I reached for it. "What are you doing here?"

Friggin' cute as hell, the little guy or girl crawled right into my palm, no more than teacup-sized. Pressing him to my chest, I studied to see if he was hurt since he whimpered, but got nothing but licks to my fingers.

"You must have just been lonely, huh?" I asked him, smiling as he pushed his head into my hand. Whatever bothered him before he seemed to be okay now. Standing, I considered a game plan for him, but I lost the thought at the sound of moans.

And two bodies.

One in particular was on her knees, a girl with bright red hair as she bobbed back and forth. I saw her easily between the spaces of several boats ahead, and cradling the puppy, I pretty quickly made out who exactly she bobbed back and forth *on.*

He stared right at me, a sandy blond with electric green eyes and a grin for days. He grinned at me, cradling this girl's head while she sucked him off right in front of me. He so obviously knew I was watching, cocky about it. He merely tipped his chin at me before going back to the redhead, those eyes of his falling back into ecstasy, and disgusted, I stepped back. The puppy wriggled in my hands, and completely thrown from what I'd just seen, I accidentally let it loose.

"Hey, hey!" I whisper-shouted, chasing it through the house. I lost sight of it between two boats and cursed before giving up and going back for my bag. I managed to avoid the couple the second time, but I did hear a groan as I made my way back to the boathouse doors.

I slammed it shut behind me, hoping I scared the shit out of whoever they were, whoever he was.

*Arrogant ass.*

The fucker actually grinned at me, my head shaking as I returned to the quad and went back to the administrative building. I returned to the simian bust, and when my name was called, I turned.

An extremely tall girl made her way down the hall, like the playing-basketball kind of tall. She had dark hair she hiked in a ponytail and didn't wear a skirt and heels like I did. She wore white basketball shoes with pleated pants, and I had a feeling any skirt they gave her might ride worse than mine.

"Sorry I'm late. You're December, right?" she asked me, waving. She had a few books in her hands, a smile on her face. "They just told me I'm supposed to take you to class."

I wondered at the "they" but figured she'd misspoken since Principal Hastings was only one man. I lifted a hand. "Yeah, that's me and no problem. I haven't been waiting long."

Technically, this was true considering my little detour. Fighting myself from cringing at the show before, I shook the tall girl's hand.

"I'm Birdie Arnold," she introduced, and I smiled, loving her original name. I hadn't heard that one before, cute. She grinned. "I'm a senior like you. You ready for class? It's mine too. Second period English."

Happy to at least know one person, I followed her across the quad to our English class. The class had already started, but I think the teacher, Mr. Pool, had been warned about my arrival, so he didn't give us a hard time about it. He introduced me to the class of about twenty-five or so, then Birdie and I took seats off to the side. The room settled for about two seconds before the door opened again, and a familiar face sauntered himself into the room, looking thoroughly satisfied with his chiseled jaw and thoroughly tousled hair like he just had a round in the sheets. Who knew what he and the redhead did before I got there.

His strands of spun gold complemented a clean-shaven face. This guy's cheekbones could cut glass and I think he knew it. Stopping the class in conversation, he came fully equipped with a note folded between two fingers, one he passed off to Mr. Pool without breaking his stride.

"A late pass from the headmaster," the guy informed, that smile of his hiking before he ventured to the back of the classroom. Pulling off his blazer, he exposed a set of chiseled biceps and similar forearms when he rolled up his sleeves. He concluded by loosening his tie. Second period English was apparently this guy's relaxation period. Once he finally made it to his seat, he clasped hands with not one but several guys in the back. Those who didn't get handshakes got fist bumps, and Mr. Pool merely shook his head at the spectacle.

"I'd expect nothing else, Mr. Prinze," he said, huffing before tossing the pass on his desk. "If you're done?"

Mr. Prinze gave him the floor, nodding like he led the class instead of the teacher. What was laughable was Mr. Pool actually let him do that before going to the board and bullet-pointing today's lesson.

I pulled my English book out of my bag. "I just saw that guy," I whispered, getting Birdie's attention. Mr. Pool's back was still to us, and Birdie turned, looking to the back of the room before facing me.

"Royal?" she asked. "What was he doing?"

That guy's name would be Royal Prinze. His parents were probably pretty damn impressed with themselves too. It all seemed fitting, though, considering the way this boy owned second period English.

Lowering, I explained to Birdie quickly what I saw in the boathouse. Mr. Pool was still busy at the board, and once my story concluded, Birdie did nothing but smirk.

She lowered too. "I'm not surprised, but I'm sure you know all about that, him."

"If you'd all turn to page ninety-seven, and we'll begin our look into the Renaissance period. December, I'll touch base to see where you are in your studies later, but don't be afraid to let me know while we work today if you're lost or anything, all right?"

The attention on me, I pulled away from Birdie and what she said. Giving Mr. Pool a wave, I told him I would, and he gratefully moved on but not without me catching the eye of a certain green-eyed blond. He had his legs crossed, thick and muscular, in my direction. Pen to his lips, he flicked at it with a finger, making a silver ring flash on his right hand.

"Why would I know about him?" I asked, purposely severing his connection with me and talking to Birdie.

She frowned in my direction. "Royal Prinze?" she questioned, to which I shrugged. She tilted her head. "He's only your sister's best friend."

To: paigealltherage@webmail.com

From: emthegem@webmail.com

Subject: Checking in

Hey,

I started at Windsor Prep today. First day not bad and Dad sent me off. You mentioned Hubert, but did he take you to school every day? It makes me feel like you were some type of secret Bruce Wayne or something and failed to tell me about it. Speaking of, do you know someone named Royal Prinze? A girl at school told me you were one of his friends, but I find that hard to believe. He's nothing like you, *extremely* cocky, and he walks around the school like he owns the place. I also caught him in your school's boathouse messing around with some girl. Do you know this guy? I was told he was your best friend…

Anyway, I miss you, loser. I get it if you need space, but didn't we always say we can talk to each other? I feel like something more is going on here considering the way you ran off and your text messages at the beginning of the summer. I wish you'd just talk to me. You know I'm here, right? I'm not going anywhere, and expect these emails a lot. I won't stop sending them, and I'm not leaving this town until you come back. I owe you. I always will.

Em <3

Paige >

Mon, Jun 10, 5:08 PM

Why does it feel like you've been avoiding me?

I've been busy, Em. What do you need?

You. You've been acting super weird lately. Going MIA. Is it Dad? What's going on?

Mon, Jun 10, 10:06 PM

Hello?

Nothing's wrong. I've just been busy, okay?

Okay.

Delivered

I need you to not do this. I need space with senior year coming up and everything. Everything's cool. Just let me breathe.

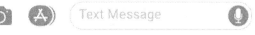

Text Message

3

The second half of the week at Windsor Prep resembled the first: lots of schoolwork I wasn't academically prepared for in an environment I slowly mucked my way through. The only difference was, I pored over past texts with my sister instead of eating lunch today. I found myself reading even more just to hear her voice in my head.

*I need space…*

What I currently did was the epitome of lack thereof, and I put my phone down, noticing a familiar face. Birdie's head hovered above about ninety percent of the lunchroom occupants, and I was surprised to see her. Outside of escorting me to my classes the first day, I hadn't seen her with the exception of second period English. We had separate lunches, so basically I'd been huffing it on my own. Not alone, she came escorted with two other girls of a similar height, the three easily gliding through the crowded lunchroom. I waved and their party redirected in my direction, all three placing their lunch trays down at arrival.

"Mind if we sit with you?" Birdie asked, her big curly ponytail swaying. "My lunch just got switched, and Kiki and Shakira have this lunch too."

Definitely not opposed to friendships on this lonely island, I scooted to appease long limbs. I'd ask what she and her friends were into, but considering all three of them wore basketball shoes and one of them even wore a pair of tiny basketballs as earrings, I figured to avoid what was no doubt a cliché question amongst the three.

"Thank God," I chose instead. I moved my tray for more room. "I seriously was considering eating in the bathroom." Day one and two of the new girl eating by herself? Completely okay, but doing so over three days in rocked a new kind of pathetic.

Birdie and her friends laughed at this, Kiki an Asian girl with a face full of freckles and Shakira a dark-skin beauty with her hair in tight twists. All three had a few questions about my full plate of Skittles, Pop-Tarts, apples, and tofu, which I easily explained. I had to get my snack and sugar fix here at school since Dad had basically shut that ship down.

"Vegan, huh?" Shakira questioned after I explained my lunch choices. "Couldn't do it."

"I love my meat too damn much." Kiki chomped a large bite out of her burger, and Birdie did the same but apologized for the display of burgers and chicken fries before me. I told them that didn't bother me, used to pretty much all my friends not being vegan back home. Also, since my choice for being vegan was just as much about the health factor as helping animals, I told them that and even made them laugh when I told them I still had an appreciation for

24

the smell of bacon, Chick-fil-A, and anything with cheese but simply chose not to eat it. That made them ease up a bit about offending me, and we fell into easy conversation about my first week and how I was getting along. I had a couple pain-in-the-ass classes I knew I'd been struggling with just because of my track record at my old school, and they offered tips where they could since they'd had quite a few of my teachers over the years at the academy. Naturally, the conversation moved on to me and my sister, but I was happy it focused more on our background as siblings versus where she currently was. I didn't know anything, and I think they picked up on that pretty quick, considering my lack of information and one- or two-word answers surrounding the subject.

"You know, I never heard anything about Paige Lindquist having a sister before you came," Birdie concluded, making my chest squeeze a little that Paige kept me out of her life here just as much as she had the other way around. I always figured this town and the life she lived had been a sore spot, I supposed, considering her tumultuous relationship with our dad. Birdie dunked a chicken fry in barbecue sauce. "Are you half?"

"No," I stated, our background a weird situation. "Our mom died of cancer when I was eight and she was nine."

They frowned conjointly.

Birdie cringed. "I did know that. I'm sorry."

I waved my hand, all that a long time ago. "Anyway, Dad got a job here not long after, and both Paige and I could have gone with him, but I chose to stay in LA. A lot of memories there, I guess. Didn't want to leave."

"Who did you stay with?" Birdie asked.

"My aunt Celeste. My mom's sister. She works a lot but she was there for me." And her doing so was something I couldn't thank her more for. Single and kidless, she didn't have to take her sister's kid but she had, and even though I was pretty much raised on TV and the internet due to her work schedule as a hospital nurse, I managed to push through in the end.

I didn't mention my metaphorical bumps and bruises along the way, but either way, Birdie and the others didn't poke. Birdie offered me a French fry from her other basket, and after I took it, she brushed her hands.

"Well, I'm sure me not knowing about you had nothing to do with you but me. I wasn't really a part of your sister's 'gang.'" Birdie paused, air quoting. "She didn't actually talk to any of us."

"She didn't?"

Birdie shook her head. "We may be jocks, but our rung on the social hierarchy is far lower than hers, her and the Court."

"The Court?"

She danced a finger in the direction of a table, the center table that always had the most people regardless of my few days here. Mostly guys, they sat both *on* the table as well as the benches, and where there wasn't seating, some stood around, eating their sandwiches with their jackets off and ties loosened. The girls that were there were either under arms or in laps, like the girl who was pretty much all over the one guy who was always, *always* at the center of the centermost table.

Royal Prinze had hands on a leggy brunette, a firm hand cradling the girl's ass to keep her there. Fingers to his lips, he sat in the full conversation around him. Though, I noticed he wasn't generally part of it. He listened, an emperor on the throne, while he observed the goings-on of the kingdom around him.

"That's the Court," Birdie let me in on, her face a grimace. "The elite and exclusive boys' club of Windsor Prep."

"So it's a clique?" I asked, and chuckles surrounded me.

"Hardly," Birdie continued, facing forward. "It's basically a fraternity but in high school. They do anything they want, have anything they want, and fuck anything they want."

"Jesus."

"It doesn't stop there," Kiki joined in, swinging a leg out to stare at the table. "One word from a former member, and you can basically get into any college you want."

"And any job you want when you come back," Shakira said over yogurt. She swallowed. "Or don't. Either way, you're set for life. Here or on the outside. The Court is very influential."

"Yeah, they have a lot of clout." Deadpan, Birdie transferred her attention from that table, her smile small on me. "Anyway, they don't talk to our lot, and their group is totally official. They have a pledging process, social events, and even club rings."

"The almighty king." Kiki growled, making the group laugh when she bared teeth and put out fake claws. "They have it on their rings, and any guy around here would kill to have one."

"You said it was a boys' club, though," I stated. "How was Paige a part of that? It's not like she actually dates any of the guys."

This was obvious considering my sister's sexuality and at the question all three of the ball players sat back.

"Your sister may have been a girl, but she was a definite bro when it came to this place." Birdie picked up her burger. "First girl to play on the Windsor Prep football team, not to mention a star player on the lacrosse team. She didn't have to date the guys. She was one of them. Through and through."

"She didn't actually join their little society, did she?" I asked, all this sounding like a friggin' cult.

"Not that I know of, but if she wanted to, she definitely could have. Like I said, she was one of them."

Members of the Court left one by one, even the girls when prompted. Royal raised a hand for them to leave, and after, all that remained were himself and three guys. This always happened every lunch period...

Not like I noticed or anything.

They didn't do anything particularly special after the other guys and girls left, just chatted, and all three of the guys were in my English class with Royal as well. Something told me they probably had a lot of classes together.

"LJ, Knight, and Jax," Birdie pointed out, obviously noticing *I'd* noticed the change in seating arrangement. Peeling her gaze from me, she resumed eating her food. "His right-hand guys. They like quiet time from the fray to discuss Court business."

"Like?"

Birdie lifted her broad shoulders. "No one knows. Most of their relatives were the founding members of the Court. I guess we don't need to know. They do what they want around here."

And Paige was a part of all that.

I stared at my phone on the table, all of this information swirling around me. I felt like I knew my sister despite the pair of us growing up in separate households, but each day and passing moment seemed liked a glimpse into a life and another world that I didn't necessarily want to see. It made me feel like I didn't know her at all, disconnecting me from her.

Lunch wrapped quickly, and after dumping our plates, I left the girls, forced to continue my day on my own with few resources. I'd probably do something like invest in a recorder or something because the pacing of this place was insane. They were leagues ahead of me in something even as basic as American history, something I typically excelled at. It all left me feeling a little defeated, but I at least stayed awake, which I couldn't say for those with blood ties to the Court's founding members. In the classes I had with the guys, they either slept or talked through it, definitely throwing their weight around this place. With all I knew about them now, it seemed they could, and I idly wondered if they even had to work remotely as hard as the rest of us, me. I stayed vigilant in class and eventually got through the day. I decided to dip out the last ten minutes or so of final period, claiming I was sick and needed to see the nurse. Instead, I found myself behind the administrative offices and in the school's boathouse again. I'd come to find out the school did have a rowing team and that's where they stored the boats and equipment. I hoped, since it was towards the end of the day, it wouldn't be occupied with school getting out soon and I was right when I arrived to an empty space.

Pulling my bag off my back, I got on my knees, pulling a few apples I saved from lunch. I didn't know if this would work, but I read on the internet dogs liked apples of all things. I put a little peanut butter on them too, and no sooner had I pulled out the peanut butter packet than a little nose came sniffing from underneath a boat.

"I knew I'd find you again," I said, holding my hand out for the chocolate lab. It came quickly, stumbling over its little legs. They looked new, the puppy really small.

"Are your mom or brothers and sisters around here, little guy?" I asked, my heart about to explode from the cuteness. Finishing the apple quick, he chewed on my finger, making me laugh. He fell on his back, and I quickly discovered he was actually a she. I grinned. "Well, little girl. Let's see if we can find your mama, huh?"

Hershey, I'd decided from her obvious color, climbed right into my hand, staying there as I wandered the boathouse in search of more dogs. I held out more apples and peanut butter for bait but nothing came for the bribe. This little girl seemed very much alone.

*I'll take care of you, then.*

I had no idea how my dad would react to a new addition to his household, but I took a chance in saying not well. He could be a real tight-ass, but I wasn't leaving this puppy to fend for herself. She was so small.

I made a space for her in the bottom of my bag, using the sweater I wore today for her to burrow inside. I also gave her a bit of apple to chew on and left the top open enough to give her some good air flow until I got home.

"Do you enjoy watching people fuck?"

The voice shot through me like a honeyed dagger, rich and thick like maple syrup. Turning, I realized I was being hovered over, green eyes like pulsing daggers.

Royal had his arms raised above him, gripping a shelving unit that held oars.

"Excuse me?" I asked, trying to be brave about it. He'd cornered me here, cornered me in a place where he had been fucking, the ecstasy on his face while he had a girl on her knees. I idly wondered if that's how he looked during *similar* acts, a girl instead of below but underneath for different reasons. I thought more about that day before than I probably should have, only made worse that he was in quite a few of my classes.

And with those damn shirt sleeves rolled up.

He had them at his elbows today, the golden blond hair dusting his forearms a fine contrast to his tanned skin. We were toward the end of the day, and I noticed he'd completely relaxed, his dress shirt untucked and tie completely undone. He looked like he just got done doing a little something…

Maybe in here.

I hadn't seen him this time or I would have made myself scarce.

Royal honed in, lowering his thick arms. "I said, do you *enjoy* fucking?"

My flesh surged like bacon, unsure if he was asking me for informational purposes or proposing something. Either way, I wasn't feeling it.

I gripped my bag, Hershey inside. I didn't think he'd seen her. I'd already gotten her inside. I swallowed. "Why would you ask me that?"

"Because you're here," he said, eyes appraising the length of me. "In my space."

"Your space?"

He nodded once. "So if you're here, you either enjoy watching people fuck or enjoy fucking since that's the only thing people do in here."

Blanching, I hadn't been explained all that yet. I guess that makes sense why he was in here the other day… and maybe now.

Feeling a little stupid that I hadn't picked up on that, I tightened the hold on my bag, watching as Royal got closer.

"Which is it exactly for you, then?" he asked, rounding my side. "December, right?"

Not surprised he knew who I was considering his position in this place and his apparent connection to my sister, I stood tall.

"Neither." I started to pass him, but a clip of his shoulder halted me, his smell cool and delicious as it danced over my tongue.

He followed my shoulder up to my eyes, and never having been this close, the flecks of green were a kaleidoscope of colors, an array of broken glass in a wide sea.

"Stay out of my space," he threatened, an unmasked challenge in his whisper. He backed off. "I don't want to see you in here again."

My breath returned only after he left my breathing space and the whimpering puppy in my hands finally made me move my legs. I got Hershey and myself together, then left behind Royal, keeping my distance as much as I could, to head to the car I knew waited to take me home.

To: paigealltherage@webmail.com

From: emthegem@webmail.com

Subject: WTF


So it's your sister. Remember me? Well, let me reacquaint myself. My name is December Regina Lindquist. I'm eighteen years old this past August. I'm a senior at Windsor Preparatory Academy in Maywood Heights, population 150,000. I'm a vegan, and I miss my sister...

Now, tell me who exactly are you?


  - December
P.S. Em is mad at you. :(

Aunt Celeste called as I crossed the threshold of the house, a whimpering puppy on my back and speed in my feet. I had to convince Hubert to turn the music up in the car just so he wouldn't hear her, no doubt scaring the shit out of my little puppy. I was sure she was already traumatized enough for the day.

I knew I was.

Letting my phone ring for a second, I pulled my bag off my back.

"You have to be quiet, little girl," I soothed, unzipping her free. The moment she could she stood on her hind legs in the bag, her little tail wagging on overdrive as she sported her happy dog smile.

*Jesus, you're so cute.*

Nudging her with a finger, I answered Aunt Celeste's call in the safety of my bedroom. Traditionally, Dad didn't tend to make an appearance until at least seven o' clock, a traditional workaholic in its purest form.

I thanked the world for small favors.

Phone in hand, I stripped off my tights and heels during an Aunt Celeste check-in. She definitely wasn't one to hover, but with me being here, she'd called a time or *four* since I arrived. She just wanted to know that I was okay and didn't need anything. After all, she had pretty much raised me.

"I'm fine and things are good. I swear," I admitted, taking the time to give Hershey a little more apple from my lunch. Satisfied, she kept quiet in my bag while I pulled off my uniform and changed into street clothes. "I'm making friends."

"Well, that's good, love. Real good," she said. "And your dad? You actually see him while you've been there?"

Did I mention these two weren't each other's biggest fans? I mean, I was sure my dad didn't have many anyway, but when it came to my mom's sister, let's just say the two could be on better terms. She had a resentment even I didn't have for him for actually allowing me to stay in LA all those years ago and not taking me with him. My aunt loved me, yes, but I think a part of her really did want him to fight a little more for a relationship with me. He could have but just chose not to do so as far as she was concerned.

She not the only one, I let that roll off my back. "Yes, I've seen him."

"Mmm." She didn't sound too convinced, but again, she wasn't his biggest fan. "He's taking care of you, then? You have everything you need?"

I wouldn't mention the food thing and this was my dad's house, so I had to abide by the rules. I'd just snapped my jeans shut when a knock on the door caused me to glance over my shoulder. "Come in."

Rosanna popped her head in, the middle-aged woman with a laundry basket under her arm. "Can I get your laundry, December?"

A lot of things I had to get used to here and this was one of them. I would rather do it myself just because I didn't want to feel like someone was serving me, but I'd turned her down before and she ended up getting my stuff anyway when I'd been out.

I waved her in, and immediately, she headed to my closet knowing I kept my laundry in there. I went back to my call. "He's been fine. Working a lot, but I have everything I need."

"And no word on your sister I suppose?" she asked, and since that was true, I said nothing. In the few conversations regarding my sister, a teacher or two and of course Birdie and the other basketball players, people were asking *me* questions about her. Not the other way around. According to Birdie, my sister also had a particular clique, and it didn't seem like anyone outside of that would know anything about where she was anyway.

Definitely not enlisting the likes of Royal Prinze and the Court into the mix, I sat on my bed. "Nada. And I told you I think just me being here will be enough. If someone knows where she is or is even helping her, I'm sure word will get to her. I've been emailing her too."

"And?"

"Nothing. Who knows if she's even checking it."

I didn't feel like she was, completely cut off from my sister. I got a few more words about that from my aunt, but not many. Like Dad, she thought this whole trip was a waste of time. My sister had skipped town before, had friends what seemed like everywhere to help her and always had them. She was very sociable, the complete opposite of me and if she wanted to go off the grid for days, weeks, or even months, she could. Everyone simply believed this was just another one of her antics, and though I believed that was part of it, I still thought she'd at least reach out to me. She usually did anyway.

"Well, you're always welcome back home, and I'll be waiting," Aunt Celeste said. "And if your dad starts acting like the tool I know he is about anything, you being there or… anything, you call me. I'll get you back on a plane and pay for it myself if I have to."

Something told me her "anything" had all the reason to do with what happened several summers ago and landed me in a clinic. We'd been through a lot together, my aunt and me.

"You know you can't afford that, Aunt C," I told her, sighing. She worked a shit ton and still could barely make ends meet.

"Don't tell me what I can afford. I want you back here, both of you guys if possible. Your sister is most likely a lost cause, but that doesn't mean you have to be. I won't let him run you out too."

My stomach turned at how she'd written off Paige. Maybe if more people were doing things I was doing instead of bitching about who ran who off, she'd be here in the first place and I'd be back home. It took a second, but eventually, I convinced my aunt I was okay enough for her to let me go. I promised her I'd check in but I didn't know how soon it'd be. Frankly, I was reeling with a lot of feelings surrounding recent events, and as I found out more and more about Paige's life, the desire to stay urged even more.

"Do you have anything else, sweetheart?" Rosanna asked, her basket full as she left the closet. Since it looked like she got everything, I told her no and she went about her way…

But not before grabbing for the sweater peeking out of my bag.

Before I could stop her, puppy dog eyes made themselves appear, Hershey with her wet tongue out and a dog smile on her face.

"Oh, my. Where did you come from?" Rosanna asked, placing her basket down, and I rushed over, pulling Hershey out of the bag before she could take her.

"I found her at school," I admitted, trying to gauge her reaction to that. True, Rosanna had been nice enough since I got here and invaded, but her loyalties no doubt still resided with my dad.

Her frown let me in on that.

"Surely, you know your father doesn't really like animals, December," she stated, making me cringe. "Did he give you permission or…"

Shaking my head, I moved fingers under Hershey's ear, the puppy nudging me with her little nose. "I was going to ask. Do you know when he'll be home?"

"He's out late tonight. One of his social events."

These already old hat, I nodded. He'd gone to a few, and I hadn't even been here that long, just another thing I didn't understand about him. I continued to scratch Hershey, and though Rosanna appeared to want to say more, I watched her expression shift from mortification to warmth as she watched me play with the cutest puppy in the whole goddamn world.

"Well, he is sweet, isn't he?" she asked, coming over. Hershey easily won the housekeeper over, rolling in my arms for a belly rub from Rosanna.

"She's a she," I said, smiling. "I named her Hershey."

"That's just perfect, then, isn't it?" The words more for the dog than for me, Rosanna rubbed Hershey's belly. "Perhaps we can keep her out in the guesthouse until we warm up Mr. Lindquist. How does that sound, little one?"

My dad's guesthouse was posh as hell, this little dog was about to be set up. My heart eased. "Thank you. I'll take care of her. You won't have to do anything."

"I'm sure that won't be a problem." More puppy speak from the housekeeper. She raised a finger as she bent for her clothes basket. "I'll put an extra veggie burger on the grill for her tonight."

"She likes apples too."

"And an apple glaze." She winked, seriously my best friend right now. She had to accommodate all the healthy requests my dad forced her to make, but every once in a while, I found a few packages of individual Oreos in my bag before classes. After finding out I was vegan, she asked me about the things I could eat.

"And I'll get her some puppy food in the morning," she said. Rosanna wasn't a live-in housekeeper and did go home every night. I appreciated any help I could get.

Rosanna and I were a couple of idiots…

Hershey's howls reached the house by midnight.

I'd just fallen asleep the moment puppy dog cries that sounded like full-grown canine barks blasted into the house like an animal orchestra, launching me out of bed with true terror in my veins. I had no idea if Dad had returned from his social event yet, but if he had…

*He's going to kill me.*

The fear radiating from that, I took the steps two by two, making a circulation through the kitchen, and by the grace of God, no Rolls-Royce keys hung on the pegboard.

*Fuck, fuck, fuck…*

I shot through the back door and across the lawn. Dad might not be home, but who knew *when* he'd get home, and I had no idea if the neighbors held the same confidence I had with Rosanna. Something told me a dog ripping them out of sleep in the middle of the night wouldn't move them in my favor, and as I didn't have Rosanna to vouch for me since she went home in the evenings, I was on my own here. Bare feet padded me through a pitch-black lawn, and that might have been part of the problem considering I had a little dog in a foreign space on her own. Her freak-out was most likely completely all on me. Taking out keys, I opened the door with frantic fingers, the sight making me curse.

"What did you do?"

The puppy had ripped up her bed, completely torn to shreds. Rosanna and I had made space for her on the floor in a cardboard box with some of my dad's old clothes. Rosanna hadn't thought he'd miss them since he gave them to her for donation.

I dropped to my knees, and the moment Hershey spotted me, she bounded over the tattered sheets and fluff-filled bedding. The comforter she'd used was completely destroyed as well as the box she'd been in, the thing completely turned over on its side.

"You okay?" I asked her, the small animal whimpering when I gathered her in my arms. The moment she was there, her cries completed ceased, and I felt like a true dumbass for leaving her out here all by herself. "You're coming to my room, okay? We'll figure out something in the morning."

Upon taking her into the house, I figured the present state of the guesthouse was okay at least until morning. Dad would have no reason to go out there, and exhausted, I dragged myself through the yard and back inside. We made it upstairs with no interference from Dad since he wasn't here, and the moment I set Hershey on the bed she made herself right at home.

"You have to be quiet if you're in here, cool?" I didn't consider myself much of a dog whisperer, but the minute I climbed into the bed with her and put the sheets over us, I got nothing but silence. The room still, she even curled up into my chest, nuzzling my neck.

*Well, I guess I figured out what you needed.*

Who knew an animal of her size could create such volume, definitely not me, and closing my eyes, I put out of my mind what I'd have to do to keep her stay with me covert until I was ready. Dad really wouldn't be having it, but maybe if I explained the situation, how she was alone...

My phone buzzed once and accompanied with backlighting. Normally, I'd ignore it, so tired, but when it sounded again, then *again*, I groaned, grabbing the thing.

**Birdie:** Have you seen this?

The same came from Shakira and Kiki, who'd also texted me. We'd exchanged phone numbers earlier that day, and they all provided me a link to the same social media site. It was an account post, and though the account itself was anonymous with its meme profile picture, one of the pictures the account posted I recognized.

The picture was me, *me* with illustrated stars over my eyes and pink hearts above my head. I was outside the school but I wasn't alone.

Royal was ahead of me, the picture from earlier that day. It'd been right after he left the boathouse and I was behind him because I followed the same path out. There was a caption above us, one I read all too clearly.

STALKER.

The word was in big, bold letters, and the caption below was even more mortifying.

*New girl gives it up her first week. Looks like the Court has another fangirl.*

A puppy whimper had me blinking with cloudy eyes, Hershey when she pushed herself between me and my phone and the text messages kept coming in. Shakira and Kiki asked if it was true, and Birdie, the same.

**Birdie:** If it's not, I'm sorry this happened. Call me if you need to talk.

I dropped my phone on the bed. I didn't need to talk to her, my hands shaking. I'd only be talking to one person tomorrow, and I had a feeling he had something to do with this even if he didn't take the photo himself.

Especially considering he threatened me.

*6*

One good thing about the Court? People not only knew who they were but where they were… at *all* times. Finding Royal wasn't hard, but getting him alone? That was another story. Considering getting him alone had gotten my ass in hot water in the first place, I made it known my agenda the moment class got out, and I figured out which exactly of the campus's several athletic fields lacrosse practice was held at. From what I understood, he played there Monday through Friday after school, as he was the captain of the team.

The captain played shirtless.

Hip bones sectioned off into a divine male *V* were located directly below perfectly toned abs, also in their appropriate subsections. Dusted with blond hair that matched the tousle he had up above, this guy was a male anatomy chart and currently stood in some type of huddle in the middle of the field. All the players looked to be taking some kind of break as the coaches were off in their own huddle and various players had water bottles in their hands as well as whatever they called those lacrosse sticks. Approaching Royal at this time and in this element was definitely one hundred percent an idiot decision.

"Hey, Mr. Captain of the Lacrosse Team!"

I was an idiot. I was an idiot for shedding tears and even worst for going to sleep by them. I was an idiot for letting these people affect me and letting *him* threaten me yesterday and not doing anything about it. I was doing something about it today, and with my phone in hand, I watched as the huddle holding Royal split up and the man himself parted off from the crowd. I enjoyed watching his eyes twitch wide and his brow flick up at being called out by a virtual nobody in *his* space. I may have had one shot at this, one shot before complete social suicide, but I wasn't here for him or anyone else. I was here for Paige and anything that resulted after this moment in time was moot to me.

"Did you set this up?" I asked, charging onto the field and passing several sweaty boys. I blew past all of them, seeing nothing but red. I had my target set on the guy in the center. I shook my phone as I approached. "Did you have someone take this? Spread this shit?"

I had the meme in hand, the meme that mirrored not just that anonymous social media post but others once I followed the trail. The thing was everywhere, haunting me with illustrated starry eyes, and up in the captain's space, I entered his huddle.

All parted away, creating a scattered semicircle around Royal and me with the exception of several members of the Court I'd been informed were

LJ, Knight, and Jax. Knight was the tallest, broad and thick as he stood beside Royal, but LJ and Jax were only a fraction smaller with their varied statures. Sweaty shirts either clinging to them or on their shoulders, all three boys intimidated just as much as Royal, but I stood up to them too. I'd stand up to anyone who made a fool out of me.

"Was it one of them?" I asked Royal, eyes on his three friends. "Was this all a setup?"

By now, everyone both on *and* off the field had cellphones out, no doubt recording this thing, but I didn't care. I wanted evidence. I wanted footage as I handed this guy his ass for what he did.

Royal's eyes narrowed, arms braced across his muscled chest. "What are you going on about, December?"

"How about you tell the truth?" I challenged, my breath hiking when my rapidly beating chest brushed his damp and completely naked one. I smelled him in his rawest form this close, hot and entirely too male. I wet my lips. "Tell them how it's the other way around. How for some reason *you* tend to be wherever I am."

Fists raised to cover oohs and chuckles from tall jocks, Royal put in his place and mocked by everyone but his loyal brood. LJ, Knight, and Jax merely looked at him, and so focused on their reactions, I hadn't gotten Royal's himself.

Otherwise, I would have picked up on the fire in his eyes.

Instantly snatched up by my arm, I was pulled north, almost dropping my phone in the grass.

"Hey!" I struggled. "What the hell are you doing?"

He didn't tell me, his grip firm, and only when we were back in the school and out of earshot did he let go. We'd entered the south doors of the campus's rec center, and once inside, he forced open doors that said, Boys' Locker Room.

"Get in," he commanded, more threats in his voice that followed his point inside. I didn't necessarily like being told what to do and being told to go into a place that said *boys'* locker room even less. I crossed my arms.

Thick eyebrows descended like storm clouds. With a lift of his hand, he went inside by himself, and I was left standing in the hallway. Eventually, I raised my hands, going against my better judgment when I followed him inside. I found him lingering behind the doors, hands propped on his chiseled hips.

"Have something to say to me, say it here," he stated, a growl in his voice. "Or do you only get off hearing yourself talk when you know others are around?"

Heat charging up my neck, I noticed the same in his, a pink crushed tone to his skin. I'd gotten under it, good. I lifted my phone, showing him again. "Was this you? This meme? This bullshit?"

His eyes lifted toward the rafters when he rolled them. "I was there. How would that have been me?"

That wasn't what I asked, shaking my head. "You obviously have friends. Maybe one of those three out there."

"It wasn't." The sigh dropped his big shoulders. "We had nothing to do with that. I warned you about that place. I warned you what people do in there, and I wasn't fucking around. Obviously, someone was watching the place, caught you and me?" He feathered fingers through thick, blond locks. "They ran with it."

"And you didn't stop it."

He clicked his teeth, shaking his head. "Not my problem, princess."

My adrenaline blazed but in a different way, hurt and the line of pain versus anger blurred so quickly I couldn't see straight. I couldn't *breathe*, and it was all his fault.

My jaw moved, my body... shaking. "You're an asshole."

"And we're done?" he backed up, hands still on his hips. "I told you what you wanted to know. It wasn't me, Em."

The word stopped me, my name cut off but only in a way I'd heard from one other person. That person was my sister, the one who left me here.

I dampened my lips. "Are you really telling the truth? You honestly had nothing to do with the meme?"

So obviously over this line of questioning again, he shook tousled locks. "Why would I lie? I can get any girl I want in this place."

*Ouch.*

We had differences between us, the captain of the lacrosse team and me. He was the leader of the school, so what would he want with a new girl from a different school? I was a nobody to him, the dirt on his cleats.

I fixed my stance, the only thing I could do to avoid feeling small. "Since this is all so trivial to you, then," I said. "My reputation and all that. Is it too much to ask if you'd shut these rumors down? You know, since you can get any girl you want?"

A consideration moved over those starkly green eyes I watched start at my lips. He moved with his stare, his gaze chasing a path up to my eyes as he closed the distance between us.

"Is that what you want?" he asked, getting into my personal space. He had a tendency of doing that, but unlike other times, I didn't step down.

I raised my chin. "Not if I have to give you something for it." I may not be from this place, this world like he was, but I didn't come here without street smarts of my own. I was starting to pick up pretty quick on these games he liked to play.

And I wasn't playing them.

His head tilted. "Consider it done," he said, surprising me. I'd actually been right in this case.

Thank God.

A small smile curled his full lips. "And this one's free of charge… this time." He left me with that, opening the doors for me but something distracted me before I could follow him. The boys had a corkboard by the door to the coaches' offices, photos on it.

It was there I spotted Paige.

Chills lining my skin, I'd felt like she'd almost found me. I wasn't even supposed to be in here, basically dragged. Had I not been in here, I never even would have seen this.

I approached the wall, my sister in several photos. Some of them were in this very room. My sister was in the locker room with boys—well, one in particular.

Royal had his arm around her, the pair doing peace signs while someone else had taken the picture. They wore lacrosse jerseys, lacrosse sticks in their hands, and I felt like someone gave me a peek into what seemed like ancient history. It really felt like I hadn't seen my sister in so long but here she was, and the snapshot in time didn't stop there. She had lots of pictures with Royal, some of them out on the field. One in particular, they grinned like a couple of assholes, flipping off the camera with their tongues out. This one wasn't that long ago, though. Her hair cut short, Paige had only been wearing that particular style since junior year, a pixie cut with hair just as dark and flat like mine. The only major difference between us beyond our hair was her lanky height and trim build.

And I guess the fact that her best friend was captain of the lacrosse team.

The open doors behind me closed slowly, Royal. He'd let go to join me by the photo wall. He was a part of many of these photos as well as his friends LJ, Knight, and Jax. Their group all had quite a few photos with Paige too. She was usually at the center of their posse. One of them, they were all dirty and messy on the field, their group holding up a trophy with mud splashed on their faces and shins.

"I heard you guys were friends." I faced him, his eyes on the photo wall.

They narrowed. "Not all rumors are fake," he said, deadpan.

I touched a photo. "This wasn't that long ago," I explained, knowing when my sister got that haircut. I turned. "Has she been in contact with you? I haven't talked to her since the beginning of last summer."

If he was her teammate, *her friend*, he might have the answers I was looking for. She had to have told someone something about where she was going, and if she hadn't told me, why not her friend?

Royal said nothing, eyes scanning the wall like a mathematician riddled over a sum. He'd merely parted his lips before the door blasted open and a couple of boys came in, basketballs under their arms.

They froze upon seeing us.

"Fuck, Royal. Sorry. Didn't know you were in here," one said, actually apologizing to him for some reason. They both blinked in my direction.

"Stalker," they said together, laughing, and my chest squeezing, I was immediately blasted back into the reasons I approached the lacrosse captain.

If not for Royal that was.

"Hey? Shut the fuck up," he commanded, tossing a slap at the large guy's chest. He directed a finger. "Don't say that. Not about her."

Blinking, I stood ramrod straight. Not fifteen minutes ago this boy wanted nothing to do with my defense. I mean, before our agreement. Totally holding up his end, he pushed the second guy. "Now get the fuck out of here."

Fear shrunk boys at least half a foot in height taller than him, the two grabbing each other before backing up.

"Sorry, Royal."

"Say sorry *to her*." Royal's finger didn't leave my direction. "And fuck that meme. It's not true. Tell all your friends that."

The boys faced me, mumbled *sorry*s falling from their lips as they turned and ran like scared little bitches. I'd be a little intimated by Royal myself if the words exchanged hadn't been in my defense.

*Jesus.*

Royal really had a firm hand around here, one that people definitely reacted to. He opened the double doors. "Come on before someone else comes in here and starts more shit."

I peeled myself away from my sister's photos, moving under his arm. In this case, I supposed it'd be smart to take his direction.

To: paigealltherage@webmail.com

From: emthegem@webmail.com


Subject: Royal


Your friend Royal stood up for me today. He didn't
have to, but he did and it was actually pretty cool.
Scary, but pretty cool. I get the feeling he scares a lot
of people. Did he scare you? Is that why you're
friends? Because you'd rather be with the guy than
against him? I saw pictures of you two today as well.
You didn't look scared of him. He looked like he was
your friend. In fact, you two looked really close, P,
and it kind of makes me wonder why you never
mentioned the guy. I told you pretty much everything
about my life, but the longer I'm here I'm finding out
so much about you. Like how you ruled this place like
the badass you are. I heard you were the first girl on
the football team? I mean, what? That's awesome and
I never would have known. Why didn't you tell me?
Whenever you came to LA to see me, you were pretty
broken. You'd never admit that, of course, playing it
off like you were there for me and to take care of me
but I knew. Especially your last few visits before you
ghosted me…

Did something happen at school? Something outside
of Dad and with your friends? Who was protecting
you here while you were so busy taking care of me
and my mistakes for so long? Was it Royal?

Was it anyone?

\- Em

P.S. Hearts you more.

Rosanna urged me to tell my dad about Hershey that evening before she went home for the night, and I agreed with her. I could only keep an entirely too adorable puppy quiet for so long before she immersed herself into my dad's radar. I figured getting ahead of that would be best, and the moment I heard the garage door close that night, I ventured downstairs to intercept him before he could get too comfortable. Over the day, I considered he may give me what I want just to get out of his face so he could eat dinner. I had no data to back this theory up, of course, but it could be worth a shot.

"Dad?" I questioned, knowing my incriminating evidence was already upstairs. I hoped to God Hershey could stay quiet at least until I told him. I'd given her apples and peanut butter on top of her puppy food to keep her preoccupied. I wrestled with my hands. "You think we can talk…"

"I got you a job," he stated, filing through the mail on the counter.

I believed I'd heard him wrong.

"Sorry?" I asked, coming into the kitchen.

He gazed up at me. "I said I got you a job. Staff at the local community center. You'll be doing maintenance and cleaning amongst other things."

He hadn't asked me about a job, nor had I said I had any desire for one. If anything, I'd be too busy once school got in the thick of things considering the curriculum.

"Why?" I dared to ask, and when my father looked at me the way he did, I thought to rethink the question. "I just mean, I *just* started school and—"

"This will keep things balanced for you," he said, nodding with it and his sports jacket over his arm. "Keep you focused and out of trouble. We're not going to have a repeat of what happened out in LA. Not while you're under my roof."

I fought myself from cringing at the statement, one mistake branding me for life when it came to him. It'd been a big one, one I owned up to but still. Did he have to hold it over my head? I'd already done that enough to myself in the past.

I rubbed my arm. "Dad, I really don't have time for a job." On top of starting at a new school, I'd already dealt with a mini crisis. I had no idea if Royal stepping in would work for me, but I knew I'd still be dealing with some type of repercussions from it. Whatever that may be, I really didn't feel I needed another thing in my life.

Dad barely acknowledged what I said, flicking through pieces of mail one by one. "You're starting a job, December, and maybe, unlike your sister, you'll actually keep one. It'll also give you some spending money. I don't mind giving you money for the things you want while you're here, but if you work, I won't mind giving it to you even less."

Giving up, I nodded. What he said was fair enough, and I would need things for Hershey if she was staying with me. I mean, if he said yes to her staying here and all that.

I *didn't* like how he'd basically made this decision for me, but it was fair, and back home, I did have a job. Usually, I just did a bunch a bullshit at the convenience store I worked at because the owner had been a joke and the employees did whatever they wanted. It had allowed me spending money, though, and a place to smoke out of my aunt's house. She didn't particularly enjoy that I smoked weed, but what aunt would?

"When do I start?" I asked, gripping a chair at the bar, and his mail filtered through, my dad tossed it on the counter.

"Tomorrow morning," he said. "First thing."

Tomorrow morning consisted of the butt-crack of dawn, Hershey licking me awake in the end after I ignored my alarm for the snooze button three times. Saturday mornings shouldn't be like this, early, but for the sake of avoiding the wrath of my dad, I got my ass up and got going. I took a shower, got dressed, and after getting my dog set up with breakfast in the guesthouse, I left Hershey to her own devices. I shot a text to Rosanna to poke in on her from time to time since she'd be coming in later today and prayed to

God Dad didn't decide to do something rogue like go out there. He'd have no reason to do so, but stranger things...

I stood in front of the pegboard that held the keys to my dad's cars, a piece of Pop-Tart from my secret stash clamped between my teeth. Dad said I could take any car outside of his Rolls to work this morning.

Plucking a set of Range Rover keys, I headed to the garage and opened the door, closing myself inside the brand-new vehicle. Dad had just bought this car last year.

I saw it in my sister's pictures.

Frozen by the information, I smoothed my hand over the wheel, the ghost of my sister, Paige, in this car. This was *her* car, something she didn't even take with her.

*Gosh, I wish you'd come home.*

She had to be staying with friends or maybe just traveling. My sister sent me photos from all over the place when she was in the thick of it from something Dad did or Dad said. She was good at staying off the radar and if she didn't want to be found, she wouldn't be.

Sighing, I opened the garage door. I got myself buckled in, then started the car. Once in gear, I let the car's navigation take me to the community center and was on autopilot virtually the whole way. I kept envisioning my sister in this car, my sister driving these streets, and my sister in this life. It was like I was playing placeholder for her, here in her place until she came back. Turning the wheel, I continued playing the game. I was determined to stay here until she got her shit together. She couldn't run forever, hide, and I knew this from personal experience. My father reminded me I once had my own shit to deal with and I had dealt with it. Paige had been there for me way back when, and this was me being there for her now.

The car's navigation literally took me out to the middle of farm country, but when traffic picked up, I knew I was in the right place. Cars everywhere, the roads leading up to the community center were a complete cluster-fuck.

*What the hell?*

When Dad said "community center," I figured he meant a busted-down YMCA smack-dab in the middle of downtown, not some glass-encased fortress in the middle of cornfields, but that's exactly what I found. I followed the traffic flow to the back, the lot just as jam-packed.

*Jesus.*

The inside wasn't any different, a crystal palace of wide windows and open space. People rushed around inside, some in uniforms, others not, but all raced to get to various activities, some of which I passed as I wandered the place aimlessly.

I nibbled a Pop-Tart, catching games of basketball, volleyball, and even bowling at one point. Virtually all the rooms were filled, the stands as well with who had to be parents.

I shook my head, the culture completely different.

*What else is new?*

I felt like a fish out of water at the school, so why not in the community too? I gripped my bag, thinking I needed to find some kind of information center like when attending a concert at an arena. This basically the same thing, I stood on my tiptoes in search of one. My gaze stopped immediately on extended height, a boy coming directly at me through the crowd. I knew this boy from school or at least knew of him. LJ, *Royal's friend LJ*, was a tall blond of extraordinary height and the same went for his build. Arms thick and shoulders bulky, he currently had that long blond hair of his cinched at the top of his head, a red shirt over his arm that matched the one he wore. He came right at me, stopping me in my path. The name *Lance J.* was embroidered in yellow thread on his right pec, one that very much twitched when he stopped.

He frowned right at me. "You're late, Lindquist."

Holy shit, he waiting for me. I mean, he did come right to me, but this was a surprise. He clearly worked here, and when he put the other red shirt he had over my shoulder, he let me know he was here to help me on my first day of work.

He put out his hand. "I'm Lance. Lance Johnson but everyone calls me LJ. I manage here, so I'm showing you around."

As I hadn't officially met him, I took his hand, shaking. Though, it was all rather awkward considering we did both know each other from school.

*And you called his friend out yesterday.*

All that not far enough in the past, my smile was stiff as I let go, and obviously, the exclusive Court ran the community center *as well* as the school.

*Obviously.*

I nodded at him, taking back my hand. I really couldn't get away from these guys, and I idly wondered if Royal was bopping around someplace too. Not brave enough to ask, I took my shirt off my shoulder and followed his extended height through the cluster of people. LJ directed me to a locker room designated for female staff, and after dropping my stuff off and changing, I joined him on the floor.

"I'll be with you until you get things," he said, pointing out various areas and the events that were typically held in them. "But even after, you only answer to me. I'm your direct manager so if you have any questions you come see me."

Apparently, he owned me as well, and I bit back a few choice words for my dad. How in the entire fuck did he manage to find a job for me under the direct hand of the Court? I shook my head, grateful at least that, though LJ was firm, he wasn't an asshole about the way he said and showed me things. He really was just my manager, so at least I had that. Had I been under someone like Royal Prinze, I had a feeling all this "showing me around" wouldn't be without his bite or familiar threats. LJ, on the other hand, was definitely a lot more laid-back, and after handing me a broom and wash rag, he showed me where I'd be cleaning floors and wiping down mats. I got to play janitor for minimum wage, and I showcased it in each and every room he showed me. I wasn't the only red shirt doing bitch work, but I was the only girl. They may have had a female locker room, but the lack of female staff was very obvious. In fact, the only members of the opposite sex around here tended to be the actual members either working out here or participating in activities.

"Last room for today," LJ said to me around three thirty. At this point, I'd been on my feet since basically 7 AM and had the backache to prove it. LJ had me doing various jobs both inside and outside all day, and I felt it.

Working out my backache, I bent into cleaning up the mess from yet another spectator around this place. I'd cleaned up enough scattered popcorn and Skittles to get me through the final semesters of high school, and LJ gratefully didn't hover. He tended to just check in on me from time to time while he did whatever he did as manager. From what I'd gathered, that typically consisted of socializing and flirting with the various female members, a job that he got right into while I cleaned my "last room for the day."

Peering over the broomstick, the tall blond was called over by a couple of girls in unitards. Apparently, we were in the tumbling room, half-naked girls doing somersaults and dance routines on the mats. LJ wasn't watching the show, but didn't stand by idle when one of the girls waved at him. He gathered her by the waist and joined a group of guys who messed around by the mats. I assumed they were Court and one of them was actually standing on a chair and dancing. He swayed his hips to the girls' music who currently danced a floor routine, and I recognized him as Jax, a practical joker apparently both in and outside of class. Days didn't pass where classes sometimes stopped entirely just for our teachers to reel him in. He had a tendency of getting people super amped and was proving to do the same today. Obnoxious, he fell off the chair in the middle of the girls' routine, which *of course* made all the girls laugh. This received nothing but a jostle from LJ after he helped him up, but at least, another guy slapped him on the back of the head for being an idiot. I recognized him too, mostly because he was a colossal giant. Knight Reed had to be a defender on the lacrosse team, had to with his force.

"Stop dicking around."

How I failed to notice the guys' leader before, I didn't know. Perhaps, it'd been Jax's dance but Royal Prinze, the one who spoke, sat right up front for the show. In a folding chair, Royal had himself lounged back, yet another girl sprawled across his lap, and this one stole my attention due not just to the fact she was half-naked like the other girls, but her particular hairstyle.

She'd rocked the same one when she'd been sucking Royal off.

I hadn't seen the redhead since that day. Really, Royal seemed to have a different chick every day of the week in the lunchroom, but today, she had all his attention. He rubbed her back while he chided Jax, then squeezed her hip as the group settled down. Eventually, she got up to go back to the floor in her bright unitard, and he smacked her ass, making her giggle. LJ came over to Royal's side once Royal was freed up, and the two fist-bumped.

*At least Royal doesn't seem to work here.*

I thanked the world for small favors, trying not to watch the group, but that was made hard when after they bumped fists, LJ bent down and said something in Royal's ear. Whatever it was made the sandy blond's head turn, Royal looking right at me when he turned fully around in his chair. He tipped his chin at me, smiling a little before he was called ahead by the redhead. LJ must have told him I was here, and Royal wanted to make sure I saw him for whatever reason.

I really didn't know what to make of that, but let's just say, my last room of the day I got through quicker than the others.

I didn't have to work the next day due to it being Sunday and the community center being closed, but after school, I worked the next few days for three- to four-hour shifts at the Maywood Heights Community Center. Hubert dropped me off at home after school, and after a quick look over my homework, dinner, and caring for Hershey, I was right back on the road and working. LJ met me when I arrived and, dare I say, worked me harder than any guy there. He didn't take it easy on me because I was a girl and, if anything, came down on me even worse. I might not have thought anything of it, but considering the impression I'd made so far in this town and how I yelled at LJ's friend in front of a shit-ton of people...

I wiped sweat from my brow, shoveling dog poo into tiny sacks. The community center had a dog park, and I got the "joy" of working that today.

*Fuck me.*

My phone buzzed, and I knew it wasn't Aunt Celeste since I was at work. She was aware of my new schedule and didn't tend to bother me during a shift. She also loved the fact that Dad was making me work not even a month into moving to a new town... not.

**Birdie:** Hey. Can you hang out later? The girls and I plan to pop your party cherry. ;)

I was stinky and I was tired, but I was also eighteen and hadn't done anything remotely social *since* leaving LA.

**Me:** Save me.

Half the Windsor Prep female basketball team picked me up later that night, a cool blue Hummer their ride of choice. Apparently, Shakira's dad was out of town, and she had full access to any one of the bazillion and a half cars she had in her parents' garage. I'd been told her dad owned a car dealership, but even outside of that, these girls had exotic cars guys in rap videos would salivate to have. I'd seen them, another world completely on the opposite side of mine.

I eased off of leather seats, adjusting the skirt of a dress that road up my ass just as bad as my uniform. I paired my dress with a leather jacket and black boots, ready to party and get out of my head a little. I'd spent entirely too much time since I'd gotten to this town either thinking about my sister or members of the Court, Royal specifically. I had no idea if he'd be here tonight, but at least with several

Amazon-sized women surrounding me, I could blend into the crowd and hopefully avoid his wrath. Birdie, in her crop top and high-waisted jeans, passed Kiki the joint we started on our way over to the party in the 'burbs, all of us already *slightly* baked before getting here. I took one last hit when passed the weed, then allowed women twice my size to slink arms around my waist and across my shoulders. They led me inside, and thank God for that, as they kept me from getting pummeled in a home already filled from wall to wall with people. I had no idea whose house this was, but there were already bodies passed out in it.

I stepped over one, a guy with his head inside a pot.

Birdie frowned. "Uh-uh, not cool, Taylor," she said, dragging me by the arm away from the sight with a laugh. "It's too early to be doing all that."

"Right?" Shakira's cheeks hollowed as she took a hit from the joint we still had. Apparently done with it, she quickly put it out in Taylor's pot, then grabbed my other arm. She pumped a fist. "Let's dance, bitches!"

Our war cries filled the house as we went down the stairs into the pit of a house inside the high hills of Maywood Heights. Surrounded by glass, the open space let in the night, and we danced beneath the stars to DJ tunes. I actually felt like a star a little bit, a shining burst of light amongst the galaxy's socialites. Don't get me wrong. I partied *hard* back in LA, but I went to an inner-city school. We partied in either musty-smelling lofts or abandoned buildings, the scene busted up by cops barely after midnight.

This was different, girls in glittery gold dresses thrusting their hips against boys with silver rings on their fingers. The Court's presence emanated through this place, but I'd yet to see Royal, LJ, Knight, and Jax. I may get lucky since LJ had been at work today just like me.

But then I saw them all over by the couches, a light burning through the air as they passed their own joint between them. They nearly all had girls, sometimes two or three under their lengthy wingspans. At the center, of course, was Royal, the last to take a hit before settling a hand on a girl in a bright pink dress. A repeat offender, I'd seen the redhead now two times with him in the span of a week. She'd been on the receiving end of the joint, smoke curling from her bright, fuchsia-colored lips before she giggled and pressed her mouth into Royal's neck.

"Ew, gag." Kiki spun me around, noticing the sight. She backed up against my hip with her arms in the air. "Might as well get a room."

"Might as well," I said, taking her hands before dancing with both Birdie and Kiki. Our party of basketball bitches sprinkled through the crowd, the tall girls easily made out.

"Try and try as she might, that's all she's going to get," Shakira quipped, nearby us. "I swear, I wish Mira would just get over herself. She's never getting Court kept."

"Court kept?" I questioned.

Shakira nodded, then pointed to some of the other girls on the dance floor, the ones thrusting all over boys from the Court considering the chrome gorilla rings on the boys' fingers. I hadn't had the pleasure of seeing one of the rings up close yet, but the form in the metal was easily an animal's bite. Shakira lowered to my level. "You see what they're wearing?" she asked, pointing at the girls with Court boys. "The necklaces?"

I did, being spun by Kiki. They wore silver chains with some kind of pendant in the center. "Yeah?"

"That's being Court kept," Shakira explained. "The bitches that aren't just sleeping around, but actually *dating* the Court boys have their own little society. They're as good as kept women, lots of them marrying one of them after high school. It's like a freaky-ass sisterhood."

I peeled my gaze off the necklaces over chests both large and small beneath slinky dresses. "And Royal never 'keeps' a girl?"

"Girl, none of them do," Shakira said. "Not Jax, Knight, or LJ either. They fuck women. That's it. They don't keep them."

I supposed I shouldn't be surprised considering the state in which I'd initially come across Mira. I hadn't known her name up until now, not that I cared. Feeling winded, I decided to take a potty break and get some air from the floor. Of course, Birdie, Kiki, and Shakira went with me, the she-wolf pack traveling in groups. I took the longest since I actually had to use the bathroom, and they waited outside as I washed my hands. I bumped a girl on my way to grab from the stack of towels, and none other than blue eyes and fiery red hair met me when I gazed up.

Mira tossed a veil of red hair over her shoulder, frowning at me when I attempted to move around her.

"Sorry," I said, grabbing the towel. Trying to make my exit quick, I barely dried my hands before having to move around her *again* to discard the towel in the designated hamper.

"You're excused," she said, her gaze lingering a little too long before shifting to her reflection in the mirror. She looked at me, though, frowning. "Do I know you from somewhere?"

Only school and, yeah, the community center. She probably hadn't noticed me, though. I shrugged, passive about it. "Probably school or something."

I really didn't want to be the reminder for her about a certain meme I'd been a part of, and when she merely nodded, I let out a breath. I'd completely fallen out of this girl's head the moment her attention went from me to the lipstick she started to apply from her purse, and I was glad for it. When she started to pull out her phone, I took advantage of a quick exit, easing out of the bathroom and nearly busted out in laughter at how awkward all that was. I told the girls about it back outside the bathroom, and as we'd *just* been talking about Mira, they laughed as well.

"That girl's a nightmare. Stay far the hell away," Birdie explained later in the kitchen. She handed us all red Solo cups filled with beer, which Kiki and Shakira tipped at us before taking back off for the dance floor. Birdie took a sip from her own. "That girl's crazy. All Court bitches are but especially that one. She's been trying to bag Royal for years. It's really some kind of pathetic."

A task she was completely engaged in right now from what I could see. Mira had returned to Royal's lap, but now, she currently had him looking at her phone screen over her shoulder. Whatever he saw made his green eyes narrow and placed a hard frown on his lips. Immediately, he pushed her off him, getting up and leaving the circle.

*What's that about?*

After looking at the phone, LJ followed, Jax and Knight pulling up the rear without even looking. I was pulled from the scene by Birdie when she took me back to the dance floor and easily forgot about all of it as I took sips between dance steps. The pair of us were just getting into dancing when some of the jocks from the lacrosse team announced beer pong out on the patio. A small group headed over there, and for something to do, Birdie and I went too. We watched the idiots outside as they played, getting completely wasted to the point of being sloppy, and I laughed, bumping into the shoulder of a girl clicking on her phone. It'd been the second time I'd run into Mira tonight, but when she gazed up this time, she smirked at me.

"Is this what you used to look like?" she asked, showing pictures she'd clearly been going over with the friends beside her. She swiped right. "You really should make your profile private."

Mira and her friends laughed, and Mira flashed her phone at me so I could see exactly what she was talking about. She'd social media stalked me, my own photos staring back at me. They were pictures taken my freshman year, photos where I was heavier than I was now. About forty extra pounds sat on hips under baggy jeans and under oversize shirts worn specifically to hide it all. They'd been photos from a long time ago and photos that triggered a very unsettling time for me but not so much because of the way I looked. In actuality, they were a constant reminder of a certain someone and times I deeply wanted to forget. My self-worth at that time hadn't been great, and because of that, I allowed someone into my life who took advantage of that. He took advantage of *me*, and all these photos did was show me that.

Had *this* been what she'd shown Royal? And had he been that put off by them he physically had to get away from her and what she'd showed him? I felt sick that I actually cared how he'd feel about how I used to look, and peering over, Birdie shot daggers in Mira's direction.

"What the fuck, Mira?" Birdie questioned. "You're stalking people now?"

Mira crossed her arms. "The only stalker is TP here, Big Bird."

Birdie's eyes narrowed. I wasn't sure if it was because of the insult or whatever acronym Mira used. Birdie frowned. "TP?"

"Trash Panda?" Mira giggled, making her friends laugh when she nudged them. She eyed me. "I saw you shoveling dog poo today at the community center, TP. That's where I realized I've seen you before. Oh, and of course that meme with Royal. Is scooping up dog crap what you do when you're not stalking him—"

Birdie pushed through to get to her, but I stopped her, able to handle this myself.

I propped hands on my hips. "I'd rather scoop shit than be caught sucking dick out in the school's boathouse. Is that what you do when you're not all over Royal like some cheap piece of ass?"

"You little cunt—"

"Ladies. Ladies." A member of Court pushed between us, but I only knew by his ring gorilla. He pulled two drinks off the beer pong table. "Why not settle this over a game?" he slurred, handing us the cups. "It's more fun that way. Whoever can drink the most wins."

Challenge accepted, I guzzled the booze without question, and a table of shots nearby, downed one of those for good measure. No one. Absolutely *no one* could beat me when it came to shit like this. I could definitely hold my liquor. We partied harder than these uppity bitches back home.

The shot burning itself like liquid fire down my throat, I slammed down both that and the beer cup, waiting for Mira to do something. By then, a nice little crowd had formed around us, and the roars sounded through the air, my name being chanted by people I'd never talked to before in my life. They apparently liked the show, and I tipped my chin to them, hands on my hips.

Not having that, Mira forced down a cup of beer. It took her a bit longer, but she got it down. After a shot that made her step back a little, she took another, the second one easier. She placed the shot glasses down, and when I went for more alcohol, my arm was grabbed by Birdie.

"Don't, December. She's not worth it."

I ripped my arm away. I wouldn't stop, not with all these people watching and what Mira had done lingering in the air. She'd showed Royal those pictures, *Royal* who could ruin my life with like, two words in this place. He literally just had to give people permission, and it'd be all over the place, my past everywhere, and if people decided to look into it more…

I drank more, put down more than I should have, and Mira didn't even wait for me to finish before she starting doing a dance of her own. I didn't think either of us saw what was happening between us, taking down shot after shot while people chanted around us. I got a lot of "Go, go, go!" but a fair amount of stops too. These came from Birdie and eventually, Shakira, Kiki, and the rest of the basketball team when the entire house joined us out on the patio.

Shaking, I forced down vomit, the nausea threatening to end this game here and now, but I wouldn't let it. I downed one more shot, almost falling over when I placed the shot glass down.

Mira didn't even grab one, and within the inebriated state of her eyes, I saw it. She'd hit her limit, maybe three shots ago, and I'd won.

I knew when she collapsed to the floor.

She literally collapsed, a gasp and a few screams in the crowd from her friends when a wasted girl fell in her glitter dress in the middle of a high-rise patio. The crowd honed in around her, myself included. Touches to her cheek and shakes couldn't even get her up, and the vomit did threaten this time, hot and harsh when it charged from my stomach but for other reasons. I started seeing visions of Mira in the hospital, visions of her dead and myself the reason.

Frantic, I started to shout to tell someone to call 911 but that stopped when four boys the size of gladiators pushed the crowd. Knight, the biggest, charged through the front, but it'd been Royal himself to create the most reaction. The crowd on the patio instantly divided for him and one look between me, the tossed-over cups on the table, and Mira sprawled out on the ground, had his lustrous eyes blazing green fire.

He instantly was on his knees with her, attempting to revive her with Jax, Knight, and LJ at his sides. He called out for one of them to call an ambulance, which they did, Jax suddenly completely serious when he got out his cell and explained the situation. The other boys pushed everyone a good few feet away from the scene, giving the pair space.

I fought through them. "Is she going to be okay?" I barely got the words out, stumbling and completely inebriated myself.

Royal saw that, instantly shooting daggers at me. "What the hell did you think you were doing? She obviously can't take as much as you."

I didn't like how he said the words, like I was that same trash Mira talked about. There'd been judgment there, me different from all of them, and feeling really sick, I could only watch as Royal Prinze slid his thick arms under Mira's body and stood with her with what was obviously a strong embrace. No effort at all came when he brought her from the floor to his chest.

"Go home, December. *Now*," he commanded, treating me like the epitome of a child. He turned away, walking with Mira back into the house, and so embarrassed, I stepped through the crowd. I didn't stick around long enough to wait for the ambulance to see if she was okay.

If I did, I would have vomited and embarrassed myself even more.

*The Past - three years ago*

"She's having a hard time down here, Rowan. A real hard time. Can't you get it through your head? Your daughter… Your daughter needs you."

I closed my eyes in my bedroom, squeezing down tears as I curled up under my sheets. Aunt Celeste went into her bedroom to take calls she didn't want me to hear, but it never worked. It was the best place *to* hear her, and my ears didn't even need to be up against the wall we shared.

"I know she made the decision to live down here. I know but she's just a kid, goddamn it. She shouldn't have to go through this alone. You know she hasn't left her bedroom for weeks?"

I hugged my body tighter, shaking through my tears.

"All right. Well, I'll just continue to raise your daughter for you, then."

I flinched at the slam down of the phone, my head touching the wall as I sobbed. The only thing that took me out of it was the creak of my bedroom door behind me, light streaming into my room from the hallway. I turned, the silhouette not my aunt but someone else.

I turned back, closing my eyes again. Stiff, I didn't move, not even when my bed sagged down and my sister put her arms around me.

"Em?" Paige whispered, her scent like lilacs. She smelled so much like Mom it hurt sometimes.

I cried some more, the will not within me to protest. I was weak. I couldn't tell my sister I didn't need her because I did. I turned in her arms when she prodded me, her hands on my face. We looked alike, my sister and me, but where she looked more like Mom, I looked like Dad.

Her dark hair she had up in a ponytail, her smile on me through that soft light from the hall.

"Why are you here again?" I asked her. She'd come for me so many times, and the reasons hadn't been because of Dad. They'd been about me, me and *my* mistakes.

Things were supposed to be different in high school, a new start and a place to be me and no longer be the girl who lost her mom to cancer. That'd followed me all the way from grade school, poor little December Lindquist who lost her mom and her whole family in one sweep. I couldn't leave LA, though. I couldn't leave Mom and the memories of her here. Dad may have been able to do that and even Paige, but I couldn't.

Things were supposed to be different.

I cradled my belly, the loss still there. I didn't think it would ever go away. I never got the chance to feel my baby, too early the doctors said, but I had felt something. I felt it deep inside my soul, and the moment it was gone, the moment I let him or her go, I felt that loss.

I sobbed again in my sister's neck. She hadn't answered my question, but she didn't have to do so. She'd been here every day leading up to the abortion and stayed many days after. She was probably so behind in school.

"I'm so stupid," I whispered. "I'm so dumb." I allowed someone to tell me I was pretty, that I *meant* something to someone when I meant nothing. I was nothing to Dean, and he showed me that the moment I told him I'd gotten pregnant. He told me I was crazy. He told me I was a liar, then called me a whore. He'd called me that when before he'd shared nothing but love, both for me and to me. He'd said he loved me and he only wanted to be with me, and I'd believed him. I did because I was weak and he showed me attention when no one else did. I wasn't just the girl with the dead mom. I wasn't the chubby girl who gained a bunch of weight after her mom died. I was just a girl he loved.

I hadn't even wanted to have sex.

"I'm so weak," I continued into my sister's neck. "I'm so…"

"The strongest person I know."

I looked up at my sister, thinking I didn't hear her right. I shook my head. "I'm not. I…"

"Did what you felt was right," she said, her face stern. "You're still here, Em. You're still staring the world right in the face, and that makes you strong."

I didn't feel strong. I felt like the worst person on the planet. I fell for a boy who used and abused me, then made the decision to abort my pregnancy after a mistake *I* made. I was selfish.

"You know, you may not believe me," Paige said, wiping my tears away. "But soon, you're not going to be in this bed. Soon, you're going to be all cried out, and you know what you'll be doing then?"

I shook my head, the tears blinking down.

She massaged my hand. "You're going to be smiling. You're going to be alive and sharing that Em smile with me and the rest of the world." She leaned in. "One day, you're going to be so far on the other side of this that the very thought of it will make you feel like it was another life and a completely different person."

I wiped my face. "How do you know?" It wasn't possible what she said, a different reality.

Paige crooked a finger under my chin. "Because I can see what you can't. I can see beyond all this and who you actually are. See right now, Em, you're burying all of it. You're hiding, but one day you won't hide. One day, you'll truly be who you're supposed to be."

I scanned her face in the soft light, still unable to fathom it. She couldn't be right. She couldn't be.

Pushing her arms over my shoulders, my sister pulled me into her, continuing to let me cry again against her. So many nights she held me like this, had to bring me back when I couldn't do so myself. She kissed the top of my head. "I see you, Em. I see what you can't see, and I always will, forever."

*The Present*

I vomited to the point of thrashing, my head deep in the toilet until nothing but stomach bile came up. I idly wondered if I should go to the hospital considering how much fluid I was losing, but the thought of seeing Mira in a hospital bed or, even worse, dead—I shut that thought down quickly. My dad would obviously find out as well. They'd call him wherever he was. He hadn't been home when the girls drove me home, but he would be eventually.

I merely flushed the toilet before I ralphed again, vomit mixed with tears. Birdie and Kiki had sat me between them while Shakira drove as quickly as she could. They hadn't even waited for the other girls on the team, texting them and telling them they'd come back for the group after they took care of me. *They* had wanted me to go to the hospital, and I hadn't even started vomiting yet. I'd obviously refused, mumbling out I'd take care of myself after I assured them I was fine and made them leave.

*Bullshit.*

I hurled again, shaking as I fell from the porcelain. On the cold tiles, I rested for a little while until I had both the confidence and stamina enough that I could hold my own weight. I couldn't, dragging myself into the tub. There, I peeled off my clothes and I couldn't even stand in the shower, merely turning on the nozzle and letting the jets hit me hard from above.

I lifted my face into them, attempting to sober myself without the proper resources. I'd gotten shit-faced before, but it'd been a while, not since I stopped feeling sorry for myself for mistakes in my past and started taking care of me for once. I dropped a bunch of weight before sophomore year, stopped the hard partying shortly after, and now, found myself a reformed drunk at eighteen, her sloppy glory days long gone, and my body felt it.

I cradled my legs, dropping my face between my knees. A blanket of fear weighed me down more than the physical discomfort from drinking. What had happened to Mira? Had the ambulance come for her in time?

Had Royal taken care of her?

I rubbed my arms, crying for the second time in a goddamn weak. I wasn't this person. I didn't *do* these things anymore, so why had I done them? I guess I wanted to prove something to Mira, myself, and everyone else tonight, but all I ended up doing was feeling like the very trash she'd emphasized tonight.

*The bitch.*

I wanted her alive, but she was still a damn bitch. Sniffling, I shut off the warm current and took the time to get on my feet. Shaking, I stepped out and grabbed my towel, wrapping it around my body. With some *extremely* attentive maneuvers, I managed to get myself dry and my hair partially so. It hung in a drippy mess on my body, curling in waves it only tended to do right out of the shower. I didn't bother with it, immediately going for clothes in my walk-in closet.

Puppy dog eyes popped out of a box instantly. Hershey had somehow gotten both herself and her dog bed out of the guesthouse, into the main house, and in my closet.

*What the hell?*

Bounding, she tipped the box over to get to me, wagging her little tail and drooling profusely with her happy dog grin. How in the entire fuck she managed to get herself up here when I'd left her out in the guesthouse I didn't know, but happy to see her, I grabbed her tight in my arms.

"What are you doing in here, little lady?"

She licked my face in response, and I did a juggling act of holding her, then getting clothes on. I settled on just an oversize shirt that hit me at the hips, the only thing I could manage to get on being basically piss-ass drunk with a dog in my arms.

"You must be Houdini or something, huh?" I crooned, rubbing my nose against Hershey's. I headed out of the closet, and the moment I sat on the bed, I got the answers I looked for.

*I brought Hershey upstairs and put her in your closet. She'd only stop whining once she was in there. Your dad got called out of town for a last-minute business conference, but I didn't want her to*

83

*bother the neighbors. Don't forget to feed and water*
*her in the morning. I hope you had a good time at the*
*party.*

A note from my ally nearly brought tears to
my eyes, Rosanna's folded note right on my pillow.
She had no idea how much I needed this damn dog
right now.

"I didn't have a good time at the party," I
murmured, letting Hershey lick my face. "I did
something really stupid at a party and might have
accidentally killed someone."

She didn't understand, of course, bounding
from my arms and onto my bed. Wanting to play, she
hunkered down in the sheets, but growled, then hid at
a sudden tap to the window. The noise scaring the shit
out of me too, I grabbed my chest, gazing over to find
a prowler outside my *second-story* window.

*What the fuck?*

I stood, heading over, but even with it being
dark outside, I easily made out a large body and
chiseled cheekbones that could cut glass. Royal
Prinze was outside my bedroom window, making a
turn motion with his hand for me to unlock it. He
frowned. "Gonna let me in, princess?"

Naked from the thighs down, I wrestled with
my clothing. "What the hell are you doing here? How
are you up here?" Like stated, I was on the second
story. This wasn't possible, and after a roll of his eyes
and no action from me, Royal took things into his
own hands when he pulled a pocket knife out of his
jeans. He used it to jiggle space under the sill, the
lock obviously faulty. Soon, he was working the
window right open, and after putting the knife away,
he started to maneuver that big body of his through
the small space.

I grabbed a pillow, covering my chest. I wasn't wearing a bra on top of not wearing panties. "What the *fuck* are you doing in here?" I growled. My desk in the way, he gripped both it and the window to push himself through and get on his feet. Once actually *in* my room, he towered in the small space, and after a quick analysis of my body, my pillow in particular, he smirked.

"You don't have anything I haven't seen or touched, princess," he said to me, completely cocky about it when he flicked blond eyebrows. "As far as how I got up here, obviously the window."

A smart-ass, I threw the pillow at him. He caught it easily, tossing it to the foot of the bed, and I folded my arms.

"You know what I mean," I said and he nodded, easing himself back against the desk.

He pushed a thumb behind. "The tree, the roof, then the window," he ticked off with long fingers. "In that order. It's how your sister snuck in and out."

"My sister?"

His head of perfectly tousled hair bobbed twice in acknowledgment. He'd obviously tossed fingers through it. He smiled. "I helped her. It's the only way she could get in and out of this place without your dad noticing. Her room was right across from his. She had to get through the guest room, this room."

His story, the intricate details as well as information about my sister, sobered me more than anything I'd done tonight. He really did know my sister, know this house *and* my dad.

He watched that move over my face, his brow flicking up when he panned past me. He pointed. "Your, um… bed's moving."

*Hershey.*

She wiggled her little nose out of the sheets, exposing herself to definitely someone she should not be exposing herself to. Especially if he did know my dad in some type of capacity. He could tell him.

Royal stood upon seeing my little dog, that cocky smile of his broadening on his face.

"A puppy," he quipped, his eyebrow arching. "Your dad let you get one of those?"

He really did know my dad. I wrestled with my hands. "No, yes. I mean, he will. I just haven't had a chance to tell him yet."

He smirked again. "He's going to love that," he said, attempting to look around me. "What's her name?"

"Hershey, but she bites, so stay away."

Hershey definitely didn't bite, but she had whimpered in all of the two times she'd been in the same vicinity with him. Something about him she clearly found threatening.

That made two of us.

I was sure it was in different ways, but Royal Prinze was definitely threatening to me, my world, and everything I'd come to know about me and my history with my sister. He may have known her and been friends with her, but I didn't know that life. I didn't know him, and yes, I found that threatening.

Ignoring me, Royal angled a hand. "She doesn't look like she bites."

"She does. Stop. She doesn't like you."

After only a quick touch of the nose, Hershey pressed her head under Royal's large palm and completely invalided my previous claims. She not only nudged him, but licked him, seeking his attention and love, and he was quick to reciprocate, genuinely smiling at her when he scratched behind her ear.

"Yeah, she's really vicious, hates me," he said, obviously being sarcastic. Playing with her, he pushed her the way I did to get her to fall on her back. Of course, she did, getting a belly rub from a boy who most definitely shouldn't be in my room. He sat on my bed with her, the two of them having a hell of a good time, but I was filled with nothing but questions.

"Why are you in here? Shouldn't you be with Mira? Is she…" Failing to get the words out, I watched him play with my puppy, eventually sitting on the bed beside him. Royal played with Hershey in silence next to me, getting her to turn and nip at his lengthy fingers.

"She's alive if that's what you're wondering," he said, Hershey nibbling on his fingers now like a chew toy. This obviously didn't bother him as he continued to tease and play with her. "She's at the hospital. I rode over in the ambulance with her."

*Jesus.*

"Is she okay, is she…" Feeling sick again, the queasiness consumed me. I thought I was going to vomit again and rummaged for a trash can.

"Hey, hey, hey. Wait a sec. Wait a sec. I got you."

Royal did have me covered, on his knees and forcing the can by the side of my bed in front of my face in quick time. Once there, I let loose in it, choking, and Royal stayed on his knees by me, holding the can while I pressed my face into it. I gripped the bed in an attempt not to fall into it and him by association. Hershey whined beside me, crying during every grunt and moan I made, but I was in no position to soothe her.

I couldn't even soothe myself.

"It's okay," came from Royal, surprisingly doing the soothing in this situation. He even did one better, his hand a fiery heat on my back when he nudged me toward the can. He held me there, keeping me steady. "Let it out. It'll only feel better."

It sucked right now, all of it did. The only thing that didn't was his hand on my back, a hand that wouldn't leave, a hand that kept me grounded and safe as I upchucked a lung in front of a pretty boy. He quite literally kept me from falling off the bed, pulling me back by the T-shirt when I finally stopped throwing up. He waited for a second, analyzing both me and the situation, and when it seemed like I wasn't going to hurl up any more stomach bile, he returned the can to the floor. The next thing I knew, he was picking up my whimpering dog from my bed.

"What are you doing with her?" I mumbled out, too disoriented to stop him. He could take my dog right from under me, and I couldn't do anything about it.

He returned with her in a box, her box from the closet. I had no idea how he knew about it. Maybe he just wandered until he found something, but quickly, my doggy was on the floor, watching from her vantage point while Royal picked up the can filled with my puke and left the room again. He returned not only with a clean can, but a wet rag.

"Get in bed, princess," he urged, nodding toward the sheets, and in no position to argue, I did, pulling my legs in and curling up on my pillow. There, Royal handed me the rag, then pulled those same sheets over my body, now raging with shivers. I couldn't keep warm, and suddenly, another blanket was on top of me too.

"Mira's fine," he said, getting it situated. It'd come from my closet, the pattern I recognized. "She's going to feel like shit for a while, but she's fine. They gave her fluids and she's already turning around."

Any relief from that fell away by my own current state, the epitome of the same shit he talked about. I was going to feel like shit too, and I had school in the morning.

I groaned, bracing the blankets he gave.

"You both were really fucking stupid," he said, and though I couldn't see him because he was behind getting these blankets on me, I heard the frustration in his deep voice. "What were you thinking, December?"

I wasn't thinking. I was being stupid. She'd trigged some old shit about me, and I wanted to make her pay. That's all there really was to it, nothing logical.

I blinked cloudy eyes, freezing when Royal was suddenly behind me. His fingers brushed my hair, and I turned, staring up into green eyes. "What are you doing?"

"You're no doubt going to puke at least three more times tonight," he said, the frown hard on his face. "I was just going to get it out of your way."

I had no idea what he meant by that, but when he eyed my damp locks on my shoulder, I found myself angling my head in his direction. I couldn't watch him, of course, unable to stare directly at him, but when he gathered my hair up in his mighty hands, a soft moan touched my lips for other reasons. Each pull and tug he made were like electrodes that shot straight into my brain, and when I opened my eyes, I saw him braiding my hair, actually braiding with precise fingers.

My lips parted. "How do you know how to do that?" I asked, his fingers quick as he looped and tugged. Done, he placed the thick braid over my shoulder.

"One of my best friends is a girl," he said, his grin slight on his full lips. He shook his head. "A girl who likes to drink like a dude. Let's just say I've done this more than a couple of times."

Paige definitely could drink. I remembered that, though my sister and I didn't often drink together since we lived separately.

I turned, Royal's gaze following up from my braid to my eyes. "How did that happen? I mean"—I paused, shaking my head—"she never mentioned you, not once."

His eyes escaped, nostrils flaring as he dampened his lips. "We grew up together, went to the same schools." He shrugged a shoulder. "I don't know. How did you make your friends?"

The same way, but my old friends weren't like him. They *weren't* him, a god at my current school and in society. I supposed he might have not always been that way, but somewhere along the way that's what he'd become.

I braced sheets to my chest. "I came to live with my dad because I hoped she'd come home. I've been emailing her, sent texts and phone calls…" The latter had stopped altogether when she basically told me to stop at the beginning of the summer. She didn't want to talk to me, anyone. Had she talked to him? Her apparent best friend? I bit my lip. "If you know where she is, please tell me. Has she called you? Are

90

you helping her? If you've had contact with her, I need to know."

I hit him with questions he didn't have to answer, and if he had been helping her keep a low profile, he probably wouldn't tell me anyway.

Royal's lips pressed tight, and when he went for my hair, it wasn't to braid it this time. He touched it, looping the end around his long finger.

"Believe me, if I could contact her, I would," he said, a pain in his voice I didn't understand. Maybe she hadn't just left me and this town. Maybe she left him too, her best friend. His swallow was hard. "I'd give anything."

I followed my hair up to his eyes. "Do you know what happened? Why she left? Was it Dad again? Were they fighting?" It always was in the past, every time she left. He was so hard on her, hard like he was on me but she was under his eye every moment of the day. Maybe he'd broken her in the end.

My hair fell from Royal's fingers when he pulled back, and I felt every inch of the space he placed between us. Gripping the bed, he shifted a little. "I just came to make sure you were okay," he said. "And if you've come for your sister, you should probably go home. She's not coming back. I know her, and... She's just not, not this time."

"Did something happen?"

"Something's always happening with her," he said, his tone stiff. "And she wouldn't want you here for it."

"Well, I'm not leaving," I said, watching him get up. "I'm not, and you tell her that." I meant my reasons behind coming here. I wouldn't go until she came back. She'd been there for me, time and time again. She brought *me* back when I was lost. She *stayed* and I would too.

Royal's jaw pierced his skin, his gaze panning to Hershey, who was up on her hind legs. She wagged her little tail, doing her dog smile at him, and he went over to her. He picked her up, cradling her close with only one hand and she looked so small near him.

He handed her to me. "Don't get your hopes up," he said, so many people saying that to me, and I was sick of it. Why shouldn't I get my hopes up?

Why did nobody else care?

This guy obviously wasn't her friend. He should care, care like me. He placed a hand to Hershey's head, then headed back to my window.

"I need you to keep Hershey a secret," I said to his back, making him stop. "I mean it. My dad doesn't know about her yet, and you obviously know how he is."

Dad *would* get rid of her. He would without preparation first or a valid argument. Neither of which I'd gotten a chance to come up with yet and wouldn't if Royal didn't keep his mouth shut.

He barely glanced over his shoulder. "I'll keep your secret, princess. But this one… this one will cost you."

Opening the window, he angled himself out, leaving me, and I shrank into the bed. I let Hershey guide me to sleep with her warmth that night, trying to forget about the other kind that had touched my back and braided my hair.

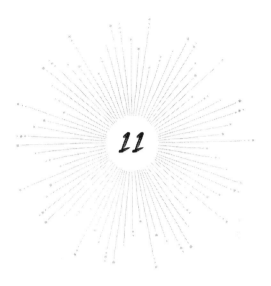

## 11

    I faked sick dozens if not dozens upon dozens of times in my academic career, but the following day at school, there was no faking. I was damn sick and had Rosanna call in for me. Dad was still away on his business trip, and she was signed up on my account as his parental backup. I stayed home that day both sleeping, recuperating, and playing with Hershey. The following, I had work, and not wanting to explain that absence, I went to school.

    That didn't mean I had to like it.

    Honestly, I anticipated how school would be after I'd challenged no doubt one of the most popular girls in school to a drink off, basically kicked her ass, then nearly killed her all in the same night. I figured there'd be whispers, stares, and still battling the effects of my own illness, I attended class with a strong headache and an aversion to any kind of food, Pop-Tarts or otherwise. I highly considered wearing sunglasses *inside*, but didn't want any more attention than I already got.

Which was a lot, by the way. I got those whispers. I got those stares, but it all also came with something else.

"Dude, that was frickin' sweet the other night," said basically the entire male swim team. They'd been heading to a meet while I'd been waiting in the hallway for Birdie. I'd texted her before school I was finally getting my ass up to go in, and she told me to wait by her locker. I did and received no less than half a dozen acknowledgments from the swim team, both men and women, shout-outs from members of the boys' basketball and baseball teams, and even a few cheerleaders.

"Thank you so much for standing up to her," a cheerleader said, patting my shoulder. By then, Birdie had found me, and when she raised her hand for a high five, I gave it to her with my jaw dropped. People were either going crazy or seriously demented in this place. I mean, I almost killed a girl.

"Are they frickin' serious right now?" I asked, receiving another pat but from some actual Court kept girls this time. They wore the necklaces Birdie had pointed out to me at the party with their uniforms. I faced Birdie. "They do know she's still in the hospital, right?" I knew because Birdie had been giving me a play-by-play via text during my time away. She'd failed to mention I'd somehow become a goddamn hero, though.

Birdie threw an arm around my shoulder, guiding me into second period English. "Girl, you're going to have to get used to it, because you're one hundred percent everyone's she-ro right now. You know, female hero?" She nudged me, easing herself

94

inside her desk while I took mine. "That asshole has been calling me Big Bird for as long as I remember, and you stood up to her."

"And nearly killed her."

She blew a raspberry. "She'll live, and you're going down in history."

"Why?"

The boys of the Court came in, Royal amongst them. Jax, LJ, and Knight made up the rear, and the entire posse collectively chilled in the back of the room.

I shrank, but definitely noticed something as Royal and the others got out their books for class. They all very much didn't take notice of me, nor did they bullshit right away in the back like they usually did. They sat quiet, waiting for Mr. Pool to start with their books and pens.

I turned, Birdie in my periphery when she leaned over.

"The Court hasn't said a word about you," she whispered, turning a little before facing me. "There's a reason people don't mess with girls like Mira. They're basically Court property and wouldn't want to test it and piss them off. You're bold, girl. They're not even messing with you."

"All right, group. Pop quiz today. Put away your books, and I'll hand out your exams."

A collective groan filtered through the classroom after Mr. Pool's announcement, but not from the back of the room. The boys put their books away, and that's when Royal's gaze slid in my direction, a silent exchange between us before he faced forward. Birdie said they wouldn't mess with me, but I wasn't so sure.

I'd been prepared for the quiz and actually did pretty well on it. Birdie couldn't say the same but pounded my fist, exclaiming she'd see me at lunch. I waited for Royal outside the classroom. I wanted to talk to him about what happened the other night, another one of his threats amongst other things. He saw me as soon as he left, but sliding on his cross-body bag, he parted off the other way with his boys, leaving me standing there in the middle of the hallway.

*Shit.*

That continued on with the rest of the day, me trying to play it cool and juggling attention while Royal deliberately avoided me. Typically, that wouldn't bother me since I did what I could not to step on his toes. Birdie was right about one thing, crossing the Court wasn't in my best interest, and somehow I'd managed to owe one of them.

I pushed through the rest of the day, but lost every opportunity to corner Royal. He was either surrounded by friends or in classes I didn't have or failed to have access to. By the end of the day, I balanced a headache stimulated from tension and my activities from a night that'd gone terribly wrong. I'd heard Mira was fine, but she was still in the hospital. She'd be back when she had strength enough was the rumor.

I slammed my locker, ending my day with a rush to the exit. I figured hiding at home for a few days would do me some good, but I had work tonight, not that I couldn't miss school anyway.

I kicked a rock by the sidewalk of student pick-up and drop-off, waiting for Hubert. He was late for some reason, and checking my phone, I confirmed that.

Dialing, I called to see what was up, and when I only got voicemail, I shot him a text.

"Lindquist?"

A black Escalade with silver rims and chrome trim had its window rolled down in front of me, a guy's hand on the wheel. The boy was none other than Knight Reed, right-hand man to Royal Prinze himself. Huge, he filled up the whole front of the cabin, staring at me over jet-black shades.

I turned, thinking he couldn't have been talking to me despite saying my name, and when I made eye contact, his eyes lifted to the ceiling of his ride.

He pulled his sunglasses off, his hair moused blades. "Yes, I just said your name, and yeah, I'm talking to you."

I stood, pressing my skirt down and feeling hesitant. "Okay?"

He rolled his eyes again, waving me over with two fingers. Looking around, I noticed a few eyes in our direction. People were probably watching me going to meet my maker.

*Not messing with me my ass.*

Braving the hell up, I approached the car, the inside smelling heavily of new car and fierce masculinity. Whoever Knight was, he had an esteemed smell about him and a ride that proclaimed expensive taste. This seemed to be the norm around here, so I wasn't surprised.

I placed my arms on the open window, and he reached over, clicking the door open.

I stepped back. "What's going on?"

"I'm here to pick you up."

"What?" I really stepped back now. "Why?"

Clearly over all this, Knight dampened thick lips. "Royal said you'd know what I was talking about. How you owed him one?"

*Fuck.*

He really was here to help me meet my maker, and where was Hubert when I needed the guy? This really was the wrong day for him to be late, and I folded my arms, shaking my head, and Knight tilted his.

"No," I said, just no. No, I wouldn't be going with him, virtually a stranger, and no, I wouldn't be giving in to whatever Royal planned for me. He thought he could just have his henchman take me someplace? The answer to that was N friggin' O.

Knight's dark eyes narrowed and didn't even say anything before shrugging a shoulder and starting the car. Hand on the gearshift, he planned to pull away without another thought.

"Wait," I said, his hand hesitating. Without another thought of my own, I opened the door and got inside.

"So that's a yes, then?" he asked, and I nodded, confirming. I had no choice but to do this. I might lose Hershey if I didn't.

Nodding to himself, Knight put the car into gear, pulling away from both the curb and prying eyes. I noticed two of those had been Birdie, and I studied her through the side-view mirror, her eyebrows knitted as a member of the high and prestigious Court pulled me away in his fancy ride.

Knight and I traveled for a long time in silence. In fact, the only words were exchanged by me when Hubert finally called me back. He told me his scheduled oil change had taken longer than expected. He apologized and said he was on his way to pick me up now, but I told him he didn't have to. I explained I found a ride home, hanging up, and after, Knight faced me.

"I'm getting you to work too, by the way," he said. "What we're doing won't take long."

"What exactly are we doing?" I asked him, putting my phone away. Though, I had texted one other person before doing so. I sent Aunt Celeste a message, mostly checking in but also alluded she should hear from me soon. If she didn't, I *knew* she'd go poking around. Call it my fail-safe since I had no idea what this with Knight and Royal was about.

Knight merely moved a hand over his leather steering wheel. I'd never been near the guy this close, and he was a colossal giant, his biceps the size of most guys' thighs. He turned. "Don't worry about it. We'll get you to work on time. LJ will fry my ass if we don't. He takes all the shit at the community center seriously since he works there."

"Wait. LJ is in on this?" I asked, and Knight nodded in response. I frowned. "Will he be wherever we're going?"

"Probably. Just sit back. This won't take long."

More questions most assuredly wouldn't get me any more answers, but "sitting back" and relaxing definitely wasn't happening either. I played on my phone for a bit but studied my environment too. I wanted to remember everything… just in case.

**Birdie:** Everything all right? I saw Knight take you away. What's up with that?

Like he knew, Knight's eyes were in the direction of my phone for a sec before returning to the road.

**Me:** Nothing. I work with LJ at the community center. Knight's just taking me to meet him and get something for work later tonight.

A lie, obviously, but as I didn't know what this was. I didn't want to alarm her more than I already was. In any case, we'd arrived at our destination…

And it was massive.

A castle straight out of Hogwarts wrapped around at least three city blocks and was completely made out of old brick like from an ancient story. It was surrounded by iron fencing, and when Knight passed through an open gate, people were outside of it, Court boys playing soccer and ultimate Frisbee in the yard. I knew they were Court by the rings. They waved a hand in the direction of Knight's SUV as he passed.

He gave a wave in return, flashing his own gorilla ring with bared teeth, and they couldn't have picked a better mascot for their posse. They definitely were "kings" around here and Knight's hands returned to the wheel as he continued up the walk and to a gate he had to type a key code into. The gate opened, and he pulled inside down a rock path, more boys socializing in what appeared to be a garden now, but there were some girls too.

*Court kept.*

Some couples held hands, others visually making out on the property grounds. We passed them all, more waves in our direction for Knight. He wasn't much of a talker, at least not to me, and we stayed silent all the way up to the castle.

The SUV doors clicked open after stopping, and I unbuckled, watching as Knight came around.

He let me out like a gentleman, or a dutiful bounty hunter.

I wasn't sure which one he was at the present.

After shutting the door, he directed me down a path and to the side door of the structure. He had to press in another code, and when he opened the door this time, he didn't go first.

He nodded me to go in, and I did, my eyes adjusting from natural light to artificial. Inside was what appeared to be some type of lounge, or a rec center of some sort, with pool tables and old-school arcade games. Nearly all had people around them, boys and all of them, absolutely *all of them*, stopped the minute they saw me. I mean, mid-point in pool, sticks freezing in hands and everything. They stood slow as Knight guided me through the room without even a stop or a glance, but I felt those eyes. They were on *me*, not him.

*Where are all the girls?*

There were none in this room, actual fear in my veins as I flanked close to Knight. Was this part of Royal's deal?

*"...this one will cost you."*

I didn't like this, on the brink of turning this train right around as boys, who both outnumbered me in actual numbers as well as size and height, stopped everything they were doing. Some rested their hands on pool cues, others stopping their games of chess and conversation. I was foreign to this place, my presence foreign to them clearly; otherwise, they wouldn't be watching so close.

"It's about time. Let's get this done. I have a shit ton to do."

The appearance of LJ normally *might* give me a sense of security. I mean, he looked out for me at the community center but here… in this place. Standing from his seat in front of a big-ass television screen, he gave Knight one of those guy handshake and hugs, only bigger than the dude in height. His hair down, LJ panned to me. "She does too. We got to go to work."

"Work. Work," Jax teased, also on that couch. He stood, the only one of the guys with a buzzed haircut. "Always gotta work."

"Well, some of us don't have daddies and mommies that hand us everything," LJ said, his eyes narrowing at their Court jester. "My mom needs all the money I bring in to her."

Shocked at least one of the members of Court and Windsor Prep wasn't affluent, I kept silent during the exchange, the two jostling each other after. Obviously, their difference of opinion on this issue didn't mean much in the end.

LJ proved that when he tossed an arm over Jax, who was significantly smaller than him. Don't get me wrong. Jax was still a tank like the rest of them, but closer in height more to me at five foot six.

"Ready?" LJ asked me, finally acknowledging me. "We'll get you loaded up, then I'll relieve Knight and take you to work."

I frowned. "Loaded up with what?"

The boy said nothing, merely winking at me before punching a fist into Knight. He also didn't answer me, flanking behind LJ, and Jax looked to follow, but I stood in his way. He was closer in height to me, and though I feared being bowled over by him too, I held my ground.

"What is this place?" I asked, noticing some of the boys around me had returned to their activities, but their observant gazes remained.

Jax grinned. "We're being rude, aren't we? Come on. Let me show you around. The guys don't need me."

LJ and Knight stood at the door I'd come in at, but when Jax waved them on, they shrugged, leaving the pair of us. I supposed they didn't need him, and when Jax motioned me to follow him, let's just say I didn't drag my feet. Any moment I could get out of this room with all these boys wouldn't be a moment too soon.

"Welcome to Windsor House," Jax introduced. Out of the room with all the boys, he'd led us into a hall, expansive walls with old wooden paneling and giant light fixtures that twinkled with bright lights. With the added sun through the skylights, it made the place kind of breathtaking. Jax's grin widened. "Consider it headquarters for the Court and all our activities. The alumni 'officially' use it for meetings and to host charity events and other shit for the city, but that's only like, once a millennium. The rest of the time, it's ours and we use it to hang out."

The place and their organization was actually legit, a real boys' club, but there were girls and I finally saw them when we traveled through the halls of Windsor House. They didn't all have boys with them, socializing amongst themselves, but they all did wear necklaces that indicated their "status" here. They were all Court kept, and upon seeing me, some of their eyes widened. I completely noticed that I, amongst all these girls, *didn't* wear a necklace, and I assumed that'd been the reason. They let their sights completely linger on me, but one person who didn't notice was Jax, and catching the eye of a friend, he stopped and greeted him with a handshake. Not knowing what to do, I basically just stood there awkwardly. Especially when Jax left to go talk to the guy and abandoned my ass.

So much for showing me around. Trying to blend in, I studied the room.

"December, right?" A girl with nut-brown hair and twinkling blue eyes joined me with a friend who didn't appear to want to be a part of this whole greeting. Sipping a red drink, the girl stared off to the side when her friend got my attention. I'd seen the girl who'd spoken to me around school. She placed a hand on her chest. "Demi Chandler. I think we have anatomy together…"

"Right." I nodded at her, hoping Jax would save me soon. Being under the observation of all these girls was no better than the boys. Especially when it came to Demi's friend. Staring off, her friend appeared to be pretty damn uncomfortable at being forced to be a part of this conversation, and she walked away, completely leaving us.

"Don't mind Jasmine," Demi said, frowning. "Her loyalties lie with Mira."

"Is she okay? Have you heard anything about her?"

"Oh, she'll be fine," Demi stated, smiling a little. "She's drama, and most of this room can't stand her. Though they won't admit it. Her family is very important to the Court."

Though I noticed she didn't say how. Reaching over, she squeezed my arm, and I noticed the necklace glistening over her chest. She was kept by someone like the rest of them, a part of this place, but she was talking to me. Her smile widened. "I just wanted to say go you. Standing up for yourself is rare in this place, and don't worry about Mira. I saw her. She'll be out of the hospital tomorrow."

Relief flooded me. "I didn't want anyone to get hurt."

"It's really okay. I'll see you at school, all right?"

I nodded, happy Mira was okay, and I really didn't want anyone hurt. Demi went off to join her friend, and by then, Jax had finally finished up with his.

He bopped over. "Ready? What kind of shit do you want to look at? Girls like libraries and crap, right? We got like five. Come on."

He showed me two, the libraries pretty badass, and I enjoyed seeing them. With the layout of this place, it *would* take me a millennium to get through it, but Jax kept up his tour. He pointed out the tennis and badminton courts from the window of the third floor, and I started to follow him to the next library when a voice gave me pause. We'd passed a room with large oak doors, and I peered inside.

"You called for me, Dad?"

Royal stood behind the doors, his academy uniform on minus the jacket and tie. He had his hands behind his back, presenting himself before a man who sat at a desk with his head down. He'd call him Dad, the man with the same sandy blond hair as himself. Though he'd had some gray in there from where I could see.

His dad didn't even look at him, continuing to jot something down on some papers. "What's this I hear about you and your friends out at Route 80 the past couple of nights?"

There was silence before Royal spoke, his hands working behind his back.

"I just…" he started, then stopped when the man faced him.

His dad's eyes narrowed. "Just nothing. You don't go out there, and I don't want to hear about it again."

Royal said nothing, his dad's threats eerily similar to the first words Royal had exchanged with me. He'd told me to stay out of somewhere before and said it just as coldly.

His dad's gaze returned to his desk. "And tell your buddies to lay off the booze. You're only eighteen, and you and your friends drink like you actually pay for anything around this place."

*Ouch.*

I gripped the doors, straining to hear more, but his dad appeared to be done because Royal nodded and turned.

I hadn't been quick enough, eyes of green pinning me in place. I'd been caught, Royal's eyes narrowing on me, and they were just as cold as his dad's had been on him.

"One more thing, Royal. I want to talk specifics for the planned events scheduled for the next few months around here."

The command raised by Royal's dad came before Royal could do anything about me, the swallow hard in Royal's throat before he turned around and returned to his dad's desk. Out of nowhere, large arms came around me, and before I knew it, the doors were being shut in my face.

"Oh, you little devil," Jax chided, a firm hand guiding me forward. "Didn't anyone ever tell you it's rude to spy?"

"I wasn't," I quipped, moving out of his hold. Obviously, this was a lie. He clearly caught me spying on Royal and his dad.

Jax smirked, shrugging. "Whatev. You just about ready? I got a text LJ and Knight are done loading you up."

I had no idea what "loading me up" consisted of, but as Jax's tour doubled back to the room of boys and their watchful eyes, I found myself too focused on that. I stayed close to my escort this time, and when he finally left that place and went outside, I grabbed him.

"What's up with all that back there?" I asked. "Those guys? They were staring."

Like Jax just noticed, he waved it off. "Don't mind them. It's probably because you're the only girl who's ever been in there."

My jaw slacked. "I am?"

"Yeah," he stated, chuckling. He threw an arm around me. "You must be real special."

Completely gobsmacked by whatever *that* meant, I let Jax guide me out to where Knight parked his Escalade. LJ and Knight were standing outside of it, but Jax and I didn't go to it. The boys led me to LJ's pickup truck, apparently how I was getting to work that evening, and the minute I saw the cargo stacked in the back, my jaw hung again.

Dog food, like literally bags upon bags were in the truck bed, the last of which another one of the Court boys dropped off when I got there. LJ pounded the guy's fist, dismissing him, and I stepped forward.

"What's all this?" I asked, blinking wide, and LJ passed me a look like it was obvious.

"We heard you had a dog," he said, pushing his thumb toward the haul. "We're hooking you up."

When I said nothing, Jax threw an arm across my shoulders again. He grinned. "She's speechless, guys."

What gave it away?

Shaking my head, my lips parted. "Uh, where did it all come from?"

"Windsor House has like twenty dogs running around this place at any given time," LJ said, coming around and slapping one of the bags. "Puppies included. You should be good to go for a while."

I circulated the haul, blown away. I placed a hand on my head. "Um, wow. Thanks, guys."

"This is Royal's doing." Knight had hands on the truck bed, not looking too pleased by the fact. He folded big arms. "Just don't come back looking for more. This is a onetime thing."

His grunt got him a nudge from Jax and a look from LJ. For whatever reason, Knight didn't want to be a part of this crusade, and the man behind it had me looking back at Windsor House. This had been Royal's doing?

*What the fuck?*

"Come on. We don't want to be late for work," LJ said, gesturing to his truck. It was a nice one, newer but definitely leagues away from what the other people seemed to drive around this town. He obviously had a different background than the other boys, like he mentioned at Windsor House.

I got inside, strapping myself in. Knight and Jax tapped us off with a pat to the truck bed, and LJ started the truck.

"By the way," LJ said, putting the truck into gear. He threw an arm over the steering wheel. "Royal said this is only the prelude to your deal."

**12**

*The Past - one year ago*

I snapped out the beach blanket over the sand, adjusting it. I'd just evened it out when my sister ripped it off the sand, then proceeded to use it as a cape as she ran down the beach.

"Hey!" I squealed, hopping to my feet. I started to run after her, but froze as she charged down to the shoreline. In her polka-dot bikini, my sister dangled my red towel over the water, and my eyes widened. "Paige, no!"

She dropped it in, sticking her tongue out at me, and I saw red. That was my only towel, and I immediately raced down the shore after her.

"What you going to do about it?" she teased, splashing me, and I dove, grabbing her and taking her with me. I dunked her with the determination of a little sibling getting revenge on her big sibling. Of course, this was futile. More skilled in the water and basically at any sport, Paige turned the tables, dunking *me* and inadvertently giving me a belly full of ocean water.

We splashed around, the two of us pretty evenly matched, and something happened while each of us attempted to drown the other...

I smiled and with so much laughter to the point that it hurt. I forgot about the stupid towel, and she forgot about playing a trick on me. We forgot it all, nothing else mattering.

*Thank God.*

I never would have thought it'd be this way, never in a million years. Over two years ago, my sister couldn't even get me out of the house, and when I finally did come out, she or anyone else had been even more hard-pressed to keep a bottle out of my hands. I'd gone down a pretty dark road after my abortion, parties and losing myself to vices. It took a while. It took a lot of time, but eventually I found myself again. I was *taking care* of myself, and now I was laughing and smiling on the beach. I'd done what my sister said I'd do all those years ago, all of this completely wild.

After our splash fest, Paige and I tired ourselves out, coming back onto the shore, and the moment Paige reached for her dry towel I cut her off.

"Uh-uh. You owe me," I said, whipping out my hand. Laughing, she tossed it to me, shaking out her hair to air-dry it. Short, she could do that, taking her turn with the towel last. In the end, we laid it out and both lay on top of it. She rested belly down, chin on her laced fingers, and I lay beside her on my back.

She nudged me. "I'm so proud of you, Em." She didn't say for what, but she didn't have to. I'd done a lot of growing these past couple years, both caring about what I put into my body as well as seeing myself in a new light. I didn't need a boy to see me a certain way. I was a badass all by myself, and I didn't need anyone's justification but my own. My new sense of self-worth only grew when Dean ended up transferring schools. There'd been pressure after rumors circulated he'd cheated on his final exams last year. I didn't know what I saw in him, but what was in the past was in the past. I'd never be able to go back to who I was before him, but that was okay. I was okay for the first time.

*"You're going to be smiling."*

I did, laying my head on my sister's shoulder. Turning, I opened a book, and she read with me, something we liked to do when going to the beach. We'd been a few times this summer since she came to stay with me before the start of our junior years. It'd been an awesome summer, the best, and even things with our dad settled down for her. She didn't fly to LA to see me as much like she did only a year or so ago. We both were growing, no longer running.

Paige turned the book page for me, and when she did, a Frisbee caught in front of our path. It nearly clipped the book, and we turned to see a girl running down the beach in a string bikini.

"Sorry about that," she said, hands on her hips. She smiled. "Wanna toss it back?"

Terrible about that, I did nothing, but Paige happily obliged. Any kind of sports was her thing, and after getting to her feet, Paige whipped the thing right at the girl. Perfect form, it went straight to her, the girl catching it before glancing over her sunglasses.

"Thanks," she said, doing a poor job in her attempt *not* to ogle my sister. Her glance lingered for definitely more than a few seconds before turning and heading back to her friends. She tossed the Frisbee back to them, but even after she did, she gave Paige more than a few peers over her shoulder.

Paige seemed to be completely oblivious to it as she returned to our wet towel, and when she popped our book back up, I pushed her. "Hey, that girl was totally eye-fucking you."

"Was she?" she asked, gazing over her shoulder. Like the girl knew, she waved at Paige, but Paige lifted her chin in that direction only briefly before going back to our book.

My eyes widened in shock. "Um, who are you and where is my sister?"

She frowned. "What do you mean?"

"I mean," I started, pulling the book away. "Since when have you ever objected to an opportunity for a casual hook-up?" My sister had a track record, one she definitely took advantage of when visiting me considering all the eye candy around LA.

She shrugged, dismissive about what I said, and my jaw nearly dropped open.

"What's with you?" I asked, eyeing her. "You've been weird all summer, not wanting to go out." We'd been to exactly two parties since she'd come, something I didn't tend to do these days but made exceptions for Paige when she rolled through. She loved them, but hadn't wanted to go out so much this summer.

Paige turned on her back, her smile coy, and seeing something was up, I attempted to tickle the information out of her.

She squealed, grabbing my hands. "Okay, okay. I'll tell you."

I stopped, ready for information, and with her smile, I knew I was about to get it.

"I met someone, okay?"

"Are you serious? The infamous Paige Lindquist settling down?"

She rolled her eyes. "We're just talking. It's new."

"How new?"

"Since last fall or something."

"Last fall!"

She pushed me. "Stop making a big deal about it. Anyway, it's nothing and probably won't even work out. We're just having fun, hanging out."

It sounded like it was more than just having fun, and I knew my sister. If she saw someone for longer than a month, it meant something, and I noticed how different she'd been all summer. She'd seemed lighter, happier.

I brought my arms around her. "Tell me more about her."

"I don't know if I want to," she said, turning within my arms. "Like I said, it probably won't work out. You know how I am."

I did. My sister was a runner, an *avoider* like me. When things got tough, she didn't tend to stick around, where I used a boy and, before that, food to get away from my feelings after our mom died. I got a handle on those things, though, and if I could change…

"Promise me you'll open your heart to this?" I asked her. "You never know what can happen unless you do."

Laughing, she threw an arm over my waist. She squeezed. "When did you become the big sister?"

"Today, when my sister decided to fall in love." I eyed her, and when she didn't say anything, my lips parted. "Paige, have you…"

She pressed a finger to my lips, and as she laid her head on my chest, I think she gave me my answer. My sister had fallen for someone.

My sister may even be in love.

**13**

About five hundred pounds… five hundred pounds of grade-A number one certified dog food was currently stored in secrecy in my dad's guesthouse. I knew because I spent half the night hiding it after I returned home from work. LJ had helped me get it in there after driving me home from work, but after that, I'd been on my own. It was good-ass stuff too, no cheap crap, and that scared me as much as made me happy. It scared me because I didn't know the reason behind the gift as well as LJ saying the food was only the prelude to my deal with Royal.

*What's Royal playing at?*

A question that plagued me the first of many days. I never approached Royal about the dog food because, honestly, I didn't know how to broach the subject. I'd had opportunities, passes in the hall, time in the lunchroom. I could have walked over, called him out like I did that day on the lacrosse field, but I held my tongue.

That's when I found the first dog toy.

It'd been in my bag, something I'd dumped out after I got home from school to do my homework. Hershey herself had actually found it, chewing on the small squeak toy, and at first, I thought maybe it'd been something Rosanna put in my bag before school. She'd been known to stick snacks in there, cookies and other contraband she knew my dad didn't like around the house but that I did like. I questioned her about the toy after I found it, and when she denied putting the thing inside my bag, that stumped me for all of about two seconds until the next day. I found another toy, a ball this time with red polka dots. It also squeaked.

I stared back at Royal, one of few people who knew I had a dog. Chatting with his friends, though, he paid no attention to the girl with a dog toy in her hand.

*He must be playing with me, some kind of sick game to scare me or something...*

That was all I could come up with and, of course, had no proof. I hadn't seen him put the toy in there, but he was the only one outside of LJ, Jax, Knight, and Rosanna who knew I had a dog. I watched the other three guys too after that. In fact, all of them for the next week, and not once had I noticed them put anything in my stuff. I even stopped carrying my bag, and that's when I found them in my chair, a tiny toy or sometimes two. There was at least one left in my seat every day, and it got to the point where my psychosis actually questioned if I had been given these maddening little gifts or not. That was until I caught a freshman in the hall, a boy slipping something into my locker. I'd been walking with Birdie, Kiki, and Shakira at the time, and the moment

116

he saw us approach, he darted off like the guilty little shit he was.

"What's that about?" Birdie asked me, more than one question I'd gotten since that day she saw me get into Knight's car. I passed it off, of course, telling her he'd just given me a ride to work, but still, she'd asked. I also noticed her looking at me a lot, which didn't help since I seemed to always be starting at Royal and his lot recently. I'd been trying to catch them in the act.

"I don't know." I shrugged, well aware all three of my friends watched as I opened my locker.

Another dog toy fell out, a thin one at my feet. It was one of those crinkling ones that rolled up like a snake.

I picked it up, determined to stop this. I didn't care if Royal knew about my dog. All this was just too much. I found myself frickin' paranoid every day, wondering what exactly the toys and dog food meant in regards to me "owing him."

As well as what he'd do in the end to collect.

A bell sounded in the hall, a warning before class started again, and leaving, the girls said they'd see me at lunch. I went to close my locker but noticed a note lodged in the vent at the top. That kid must have pushed it in with the toy.

I pulled it out, unfolding it.

*Meet me at McAlester's Pumpkin Patch tonight, eight o' clock, past the patch and outside the corn maze. Bring Hershey and the dog toys.*

He'd left no name, but he didn't have to…

He said bring Hershey.

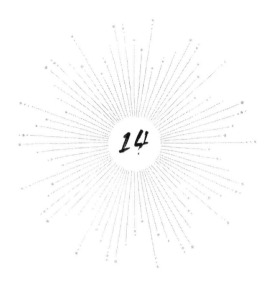

14

"Hi, niece. I just wanted to call and let you know I got a few packages back home for you today. From some colleges?"

*Shit.*

Aunt Celeste would call me during my trip out in the middle of the boonies, to see Royal with my dog wagging her tail in the front seat of my sister's Range Rover. Then again, maybe this was the perfect time for her to call me.

If I went missing, at least someone would know.

I was using her as my fail-safe again and pushed my hair behind my ear. "Can you just save them for me?"

"You don't want me to ship them out? Shouldn't you be deciding on something soon? I mean, some of these are pretty good schools, and you might be able to get a scholarship based off my income."

Christ, I really hadn't wanted to talk to her about this now with some distance between us. But some things had changed, and I bit my lip.

"I'm thinking about staying around here."

"And going to college?" She'd sounded shocked.

"Not necessarily. I think I want to just wait maybe, work? Dad's job he got me isn't so bad."

I could put up with time at the community center. LJ most likely wouldn't be there since he'd probably be off to college himself, and the job really wasn't so bad, hard work but mindless.

A sigh bled into the phone. "This is about your sister, isn't it? From what I understand, you haven't heard anything, right?"

I'd checked in with her so she knew. "Correct."

"So now, you're ruining your life over this? Putting everything on hold when all this is most likely just drama between *your dad* and your sister? He ran her off, and now, you're letting yourself get caught up in it too?"

She really wasn't my dad's biggest fan, not that I could blame her. I wasn't his either really.

My phone buzzed on my call and pulling it away, I noticed a text message. Sitting at a stop sign, I checked it out and my eyes nearly bugged out.

*"Hey, you almost here? I'm not waiting around forever. It's Royal by the way."*

Of course, it was and how the fuck did he get my number? My jaw clenched, I ignored it, going back to Aunt Celeste. I sighed, pulling away from the stop. "Aunt C…"

"You're smart, December." Her own exasperated sigh bled into the line. "You get pretty good grades. You could go somewhere and get away from all this. You could live your life for you."

My jaw moved. "Auntie, let's not talk about this now. I'm kind of in the middle of something." The sign for the pumpkin patch filled my vision with the words, the insignia highlighted with orange and yellow twinkling lights. The mascot was a scarecrow, one waving to allow people inside between two pumpkins.

"What could be more important than discussing your future, honey?"

Past the pumpkin patch was the corn maze, and outside of the rows upon rows of corn were two cars, a slick Audi and the other a dingy pickup. The one and only Royal Prinze lounged outside of the latter, his legs and arms crossed as he apparently waited for me. I pulled up beside the nicer car, putting my own into park.

"I'm meeting a friend," I said, seeing the opposite outside my window. Pushing off the truck bed, Royal approached in a tight T-shirt and well-worn jeans, and I faced forward. "It hasn't been easy to come across those lately."

A cheap shot, I knew, and had I bothered to update my aunt that I found friends since moving here, other than my older stories about those first days, she might have given me more of a hard time.

"We need to talk about this soon, okay? I won't bother you about it now. Have fun with your friend. I love you, kid."

After telling her the same, I clicked out of my seat belt, then grabbed my book bag off the floor.

"All right, get on in," I said, nudging Hershey. She was already getting a little too big for the bag, seeming to have doubled if not tripled in the short amount of time since I got her, but she managed to wrestle her puppy self inside. Her cushion was all the dog toys that I brought. I got out of the Range Rover in a blue jumper, my street clothes foreign to me considering all my time was spent in school uniforms.

I could say the same for Royal.

He approached around the back of my car, jeans way too tight and hugging his thick, no doubt lacrosse-chiseled thighs. I thought the way his dress shirts and blazers hit his broad shoulders and firm chest made him look good, but a single white tee in the middle of cornstalks made him look like a calendar ad. He looked like a farm boy, uniquely average when he was *so* not so.

"How did you get my number?" I asked, shooting off at him the moment he placed eyes on me, then my bag. Hershey inside, I squeezed it to my chest.

His eyes rolled as he pushed fingers through his hair. "I don't know. Asked around?"

"Bullshit. From who? Birdie?" She'd never give him my number, not in a million years without my permission. She and the rest of the basketball team loved how the world fawned all over him and the Court just as much as myself.

He placed a hand on the back of my car. "Your sister, I guess."

"My sister?"

He nodded. "She gave it to me one day. I don't know, for emergencies or something? The alternative was your dad, and obviously, she didn't want him called for anything." He lifted a shoulder. "I guess I've always had it."

I honestly didn't know how I felt about that, and when he got closer, I pulled my bag out of his sight, putting it on my shoulder and behind me.

"I take it Hershey's in there?"

I kept my mouth shut about that, raising my chin. "What do you want with her? You can't have her."

"I don't want her."

"So what's this about?"

"And ruin the surprise?" he said, backing away. "Come on, and did you bring the dog toys?"

At least he admitted to those to my face this time, all this entirely too weird for my liking. I told him I did, following him, but stopped. "Where are we going?"

He circulated the dingy truck, going around to the passenger side, and I followed him. He clicked it open. "We got to go deeper into the patch. We'll take this. It'll handle better than our cars in the mud out here."

Dad would most assuredly kill me for ruining any of his cars, my sister's included.

I really didn't want to do this, get in any car with him at all.

"Is all this over after tonight, then?" I asked. "Me owing you or whatever?" I meant, would he keep quiet about Hershey, and when his lips pulled together, his nod firm, he gave me that.

I got inside the truck, then quick, he closed the door behind me. I held Hershey's bag in my lap as Royal eased himself in, filling the truck's cabin with his starkly cool scent. He smelled like aftershave and boy, a really good-smelling boy, and that had me thinking about things I didn't want to think about. Things like how his hands felt on me and in my hair the night I puked my brains out in front of him. These were thoughts I definitely shouldn't have considering he might be kidnapping me right now.

Royal put the truck into gear, the truck grunting forward, but it handled really well over the divots and bumps as we got going. All the rattling caused Hershey to bark inside my bag, though, and I unzipped it wide so she could pop her head out and see what was going on.

Royal laughed at the sight of her curiosity, a deep and reverent chuckle that played harsh at my insides with how nice it sounded. He didn't laugh a lot, and the last time I'd seen him, he'd been getting lectured by his dad.

I hugged the bag. "What are we doing?"

"You'll see, and don't worry, you'll like it. Both you and Hershey."

I highly doubted that, hugging her closer. Royal had his lights on super bright, so she got a real good view of the entire ride, looking just as happy as Royal had only moments ago. The only one not here for this "fun time" was me, my anxiety through the goddamn roof. We stopped suddenly, *jarringly*, in the stick shift truck, and rather than waiting for Royal to play gentleman and let me out, I opened the door, and I hopped to the dirt myself.

"Where are the dog toys?" he asked once he joined me.

Minding Hershey, I grabbed a couple around her, handing them off to him. He took them, telling me to follow him. He had a couple tennis balls in his hands, ones that rattled when he shook them. He did that toward the cornstalks, and after he did, he just listened.

I stayed silent, a chill in the air, and really, I thought I was about to meet my maker. I was out in the middle of the perfect setting for a teen murder drama, out here with basically my arch enemy. Nothing about my history with this boy put me at any kind of ease.

Royal shook the toys again, then backed up toward me and Hershey. I opened my mouth to speak, but then...

Noses, lots of tiny noses, and yips touched the air, tiny barks that sounded so much like my little dog's. They came out of the cornstalks, not one but several puppies, and what was crazy was they *all* looked like mine, miniature chocolate labs that bounded out of the maze.

Royal threw one of the balls, and no less than three went after it. He tossed the other. "Do you have the other toys?"

Blown completely frickin' away about all this, I got more, and by then, Hershey was freaking out. She wanted to play too, and after giving Royal more dog toys, I fished her leash out of the bag. I hadn't gotten to walk with her yet, but it was something Rosanna got for her with her initial puppy food. I stared in wonder at all the dogs. "Where did they all come from?" I asked.

Grinning, Royal tossed another toy, more dogs racing after them. He bent when a couple came back with the initial toys. He faced me. "They were born here. My cousin's one of the owners of the patch. His lab just had puppies a while back."

My jaw slacked as I placed my puppy down, and the moment I did, the others descended on her. My heart leaped at first, but Hershey started wrestling with them and I laughed. I lowered, so many puppies playing and jumping on each other. I counted about eight, but really there could have been more.

Royal handed me a rope, and I played tug with one with a white-tipped tail. His grin widened. "They seem to like her."

"Yeah," I said, then had a thought. "You don't think she's one of them, do you? I didn't see any other dogs when I found her. I found her in the boathouse that first day."

His head lifted with that, and he turned, peering into the cornstalks. "It's possible. I mean, we're pretty far out from campus, but it's kind of odd you just found what looks like a purebred Labrador retriever."

One of Hershey's potential brothers or sisters tugged at the rope, my tugs a little distracted. Especially when Hershey kept trying to jump on the puppy and play with them herself. I took the rope away, letting her, and watched the two be way too cute for my heart. It made me happy, but kind of sad too for some reason.

A shoulder touched mine, Royal's when he lowered to his knees. He watched them play too as he touched a knee to the dirt.

"Should I leave her with them?" I asked him, finding his eyes. Too deep, they drowned me in their depths.

He wet his lips. "Up to you or maybe up to Hershey?" he stated, turning to the pup. His lips lifted at her. "My cousin isn't getting rid of them. They'd live their lives here together."

That thickened my throat more than it should have, and suddenly, I found myself moving away from him. This had been a part of his plan. He kept my secret about Hershey only to take her away from me after all.

I freed my puppy from her leash, giving her the option to run away. I'd done it quick so I wouldn't let myself think. I just wanted her to be happy, and though she started to run away and play with the others, she didn't get far before coming back to me. She pressed paws to my knee, wagging her tail.

"Go," I said, trying to be selfless when I nudged her. "Go play. That's your family." I guided her away, but once again, she'd get maybe a few steps before coming back. She wouldn't leave me and actually tried to climb on my leg to come back to me.

"I guess she's made her choice," Royal said, smiling at the pair of us. Taking a toy out of my bag, he tossed it. Eventually, I watched him stand and go after the other pups. He played fetch with them, even showing them tricks like sit and roll over. He knew what he was doing.

*She chose me.*

I knew it was stupid, but I wanted to break down in damn tears at that. I cradled Hershey's little face, scratching her deep behind the ears the way she liked.

"Come on. Let's play, little girl," I said, tossing a toy. I kept her unleashed, trusting her to come back, and each time she did. She never strayed, loving her good time with the others, but she always came back to me. She played her little heart out, and Royal was able to show her a few tricks as well. He got her to roll on her back before giving her a toy and even sit a couple times. By the end, she'd exhausted her damn self, and I carried a sleeping puppy in my arms to the cabin of the truck. I used the front of my bag as a dog bed for her, and no sooner had I placed her on it than she fell asleep.

"She obviously doesn't have as much stamina as them," I said, laughing at her. I closed the door silently, watching as Royal climbed in the back of the truck bed and tossed more toys.

I joined him. The two of us sat and tossed toys until there weren't any more, and eventually, we both heard a whistle. The doggies darted off in the general direction, disappearing behind the cornstalks.

"My cousin, no doubt," he said, raising a leg. "Probably called them inside the house."

"Well, they exhausted this one," I told him, laughing when I glanced inside the truck window. Hershey's tongue hung out and everything in sleep.

This made Royal's smile quirk up. His gaze found the stars, and mine did too for a while. It really was beautiful out here, open.

I panned his way. "What exactly is Route 80?" Honest to God, the words fell out of my mouth. I mean, true, I'd thought about them. More than once, and seeing Royal… I don't know. I just spoke…

I shouldn't have, and I knew the moment his fingers went to his mouth. He clamped up a bit, not how he'd been before when his jaw worked.

"So you had been spying?" he asked.

"I didn't," I lied. I pulled my arms around my legs. "I mean, I didn't mean to do it. Jax was just showing me around Windsor House. I heard."

His nod had him looking out to the stars again. "My dad's a jerk."

"I guess we share that, then."

His gaze flicked over, his expression softening a bit when he laced his fingers. "Your dad is just cold. Mine's an ass."

"Why didn't he want you to go out to that Route 80? What's out there?"

"I don't know if I should tell you."

"Why?"

Green irises shifted toward me. "Because that's the last place I saw your sister."

I froze, not what I'd been expecting him to say. "What?"

His sigh was heavy. "It's the last place I saw your sister, the last time we were together before…" His jaw moved. "Before she took off and basically told me the next day in a text. She said she was skipping town and didn't respond to any of my texts after that. Straight ghosted. Anyway, my dad doesn't want me out there because he knew *why* I was out there."

"Why were you?"

He stared off. "I guess I was doing some sentimental shit. Paige was one of my best friends." He shrugged. "I missed her, wanted to be where I last saw her, and my dad wasn't having any of that. He isn't her biggest fan. Never has been. When we were kids, we always got into trouble and, when we got older, even more. We skipped class together. Skipped town sometimes, and he just wants me to forget all that and her as he sees her as the source. She's not, though. *He* is. He and your dad. I think that's how we got to be friends. We bonded over our shitty dads."

My heart squeezed, at a complete lack of words.

His hands came together. "I owe her so much, everything. She looked out for me. My dad's a real fucking asshole, and she was always there."

I swallowed, seeing just a snapshot of that. I cradled my legs tighter. "Any idea why she left? Was it Dad?"

He wet his lips. "I wish it was this time. It's more complicated than that, though."

"How?"

He moved his legs. "There was this girl she was seeing. Made her all tense. When things were good, they were awesome, but when things were bad…" His expression hardened. "She and the situation with her ran your sister off, and I know it did. I just wish she would have stayed. We could have dealt with this, her."

"Who was the girl? Someone at school?"

He shook his head. "She doesn't matter, though. What matters is she drove your sister away. The end of all that with her and your sister went down pretty fucking shitty. I saw it, was there for it. That girl broke her damn heart, and though Paige wasn't without fault in some of it, she didn't deserve that."

"What happened between them?"

"That doesn't matter either." He braced his arms. "I just know she's not coming back. Not this time. She ripped her goddamn heart out."

Paige had mentioned a girl she'd been seeing last summer. She passed it off like it hadn't been much of a thing then, but I knew better. She'd been so lit up, then suddenly, it'd been like a switch went off. Paige's texts had become more guarded, her calls less and less. Had it been this?

Had my sister had her heart broken and I didn't even know?

Chills racked my shoulders, and I rubbed my arms. "You really don't know anything? About where she is? What about the girl she was seeing?"

"She don't know shit, and she doesn't care either." His growl brought more chills, that bite about him familiar. "Just leave all that alone. She hurt your sister, and the last thing Paige would want is you anywhere near her. She was a monster."

I covered my arms. "It sounds like you two really had each other's backs."

He said nothing, his swallow hard. "I could have had it more."

I watched that move over his face, his guard up again. Eventually, he stood to his feet, and I tilted my head.

"Should we probably get you back, then?" he asked, putting a hand on top of the truck.

I rose up. "We don't have to. Hershey's still sleeping. I wouldn't mind letting her rest."

I had no idea what the fuck I was doing, but for whatever reason, I didn't *want* to leave. I wanted to stay, be around my sister's best friend for a while.

Royal's lips parted, a clear debate in his eyes, but for whatever reason he got down to his knees and reached into the cabin through the back window. He pulled out some blankets and handed me one. "Might as well get comfortable, then. It gets chilly out here."

Nodding, I helped him spread out one blanket, and the pair of us lay on top of it. The other I wrapped around my body like a burrito while he laced hands behind his head and gazed up at the stars. The way he lay, his hands behind his head, brought form to his biceps and broad chest, a form that had me looking at him as neither an enemy nor my sister's bestie.

Swallowing, I studied the stars. "Can I ask you something?"

He turned on his side, his focus all on me.

I swallowed again. "What's with all this? Dragging me out here with Hershey and everything? How is that me owing you anything?" If anything, it all seemed kind of nice what he did.

He shrugged. "More sentimental shit, I guess. Your sister and I used to come out here all the time when we were kids, and when I heard about my cousin's pups and knew you had one just like them…" He shrugged again. "I don't know. It gave me an excuse to come out again, something to do."

*Something to do…*

I eyed him. "I mean, you could have asked anyone else out here. LJ, Jax, Knight, or any one of your friends?" And he wouldn't have had to drag them at that, blackmail them.

"Could have," he said, flashing those entirely too green irises at me. He fell to his back, tilting his chin up at the stars. "I chose you, though. Didn't I?"

*He chose me.*

My gaze found the stars then too, not knowing what else to look at. Royal moved, and when I finally did look at him, he'd repositioned, lacing fingers across his wide chest.

He grinned. "Fuck, we used to get into so much shit out here. It helped that my cousin owned the place. He let us do whatever we wanted, ride tractors, eat corn dogs until we exploded, and just chill around here until after midnight."

I smiled. "That all sounds amazing. Well, except for the corn dogs part." He faced me, and I shrugged. "I'm vegan, don't eat animal products."

One would have thought I told him I was a cannibal with the way he looked at me.

He arched an eyebrow. "You're for real with that? Like actually for real?"

132

I turned on my shoulder. "Yeah?"

His brow moved up a little before he stared ahead. "Interesting."

"Interesting?"

He smiled a little. "Just interesting."

Already having dealt with the world's awe of my personal preference for my own damn diet, I shook my head. "So you dragged me all the way out here because you didn't want to go by yourself, but also didn't want to go with one of the bazillion and a half friends you have?"

"Sometimes, being around a ton of people at any given time is overrated." He sounded dismissive about it. "Anyway, last time I took Jax, he wouldn't shut the hell up. Then, I had LJ getting on Jax because he wouldn't shut up, Knight *on him* because he was being drama." He shook his head as if recalling the night. "Sometimes, you just want the quiet."

"And the dog toys?"

"A peace offering. It's no secret you don't like me very much."

Maybe if he'd given me a reason beyond threats and a cold exterior that could challenge my dad's, that would have been different. He *made* people not like him—at least me.

I said nothing, gazing away.

"My turn for a question now, princess."

I rolled my eyes. "Yes, Mr. *Prinze*."

He chuckled. "Why the fuck are you vegan? I mean, how does that even work? How do you get your protein?"

A classic "omni" or omnivore question and one I was fully equipped to answer.

"There's protein in everything you eat," I said. "And do you have any idea how much factory farming affects the planet?"

He grinned to himself. "I'm sure you're about to tell me."

I rolled my eyes. "Just know it's bad, and I get plenty of protein." I bunched up the blanket behind my head, making a pillow. "I also care about the planet and the animals, of course."

"Of course."

I eyed him. "Then, there's the health benefits." I'd lost him at this point, but chose to keep talking. I frowned. "I'm sure you saw the pictures of what I used to look like freshman year. Mira was flashing them around at that party, and that was *before* I changed my diet, FYI…"

I bit my lip, having spoken too much after recalling how he'd left Mira after clearly seeing those pictures. He'd looked so put off then.

Royal put me out of my misery by continuing to stare at the great wide above, and I stayed silent too.

"I did the see the pictures, princess," he said after a while. "And I see you now. Same thing."

Having no idea what he meant by that, I stared right at him, but to my surprise, he already had that cool stare of his on me. He dragged me in deep wherever he was, his hands folded together while he lounged on an arm. It was a loud and vibrant sound that pulled us both out of it, and Royal sat up, gazing into the truck cabin. He chuckled. "Was that the dog?"

It sounded *again*, and I got up. Sure enough, Hershey was on her side, snoring her little heart out, and I laughed too.

"You should hear her bark," I said. "There's a full-grown dog in that little body."

"I'll fucking say." The bright lights from above touched his eyes, making them way too lustrous for their own good. They were as fiery as the stars above in the moonlight. *He* was a star and bigger than anything I could ever be. How was it someone as ordinary as my sister got wrapped up with a boy who basically ruled the world?

I think I was starting to see.

I was seeing him, and when he leaned forward, I didn't pull away. I let him brush his lips against mine. I let him pinch my chin between two fingers and guide me into his taste. He fell away quickly, eyes on nothing but my burning lips as he tugged my hair close.

"I can't." The growl I actually heard in his voice, the groan to deny further intent. He pulled back. "You're Paige's sister, off-limits."

He was Paige's best friend, also off-limits. I stared at his lips. "What should we do about it?"

He smiled, leaning in. "See if it's worth it?"

I nodded, tugging his shirt and crashing his lips against mine. He tasted like heaven and equal parts sin, his tongue delving into my mouth as he dove in for a better taste. He hovered above me, a body heavy with weight and muscle and my body humming with familiarity.

Especially when he slid a hand inside my jumper.

He'd undone the buttons so easily, his fingers rough against my quivering tummy. He stopped again then, the pads of his fingers chasing the line of my panties.

"I shouldn't do this," he said, retreating a little, but I noticed he didn't remove his hand. He touched a thumb to my belly button. "If I have more, I'm going to want more."

I wanted him to have more. Even more so since he stopped himself. I had a feeling he didn't do that a lot.

I dampened my lips, then wet his, urging him not to stop with flicks of my tongue. He covered me, pinning me under the stars, and I felt every ounce of him. I'd done this before with another boy who I thought loved me. I thought he showed me love, but realized in the end, he just wanted my body and nothing more. What's horrible was I think I knew that back then. I did but was so desperate for something outside of myself I didn't care. I let him use me because there was a sadness inside me I just wanted to go away. I took my mom's death pretty hard, and even though I stayed behind and didn't leave like Paige and my dad, I used another coping mechanism. I used a boy's false love not to feel anything.

I didn't do that now. I wanted to feel this, every touch and caress of Royal's skin a burn to my longing flesh. I wanted him. I wanted to feel him and wouldn't escape this. He'd been the first guy I'd been with since a horrible mistake I allowed to come into my life.

"Em… fuck." The shortening of my name didn't come from nowhere. This boy knew my sister, and through her, he might have known me. He did know me. He knew how I liked to be touched, kissed, as he worked my jumper off me, then later my panties and bra. He placed his hard body between my legs, and I tugged his shirt away, beautiful skin bare and tan in the wide moonlight. He was perfect, gorgeous,

136

and I kissed his chest, watching as he guided me up to his mouth.

His groan was feral, and he didn't give me another second to change my mind before he undid his pants and grabbed a condom from his jeans. Perhaps he was past that point. I think we both were. Now that I had more, I wasn't going to not have it.

The ache came the moment he pressed himself between my legs, all of this a long time for me, and the way he moved, so slow and intentional with his care, I had a feeling he thought it'd been the first time for me. I appreciated that since it had been a while, whimpering as he paced his powerful hips so slowly. He kissed me to make it easier, pulling the blanket around us and keeping me warm. I gripped his shoulder blades as I crested the high, and it didn't take long for him to join me.

He grunted and his entire body shook as he squeezed my body to give the last bit of himself. He had complete ecstasy in his eyes as he opened them, and caging my face, he didn't leave. He kissed me again, fooling me real good.

He made me feel like I was the only one.

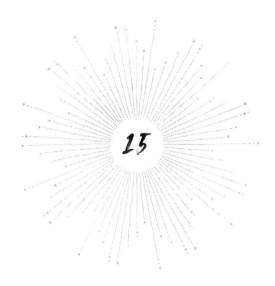

# 15

Little yips tugged me awake, tiny dog barks as they sounded above. Second came the sun, heat and a firm arm around my waist. It brought me close, possessive and warm as I was pulled back into a bare chest. A sheet of unyielding muscle surrounded me, Royal's hold so, so tight. We stayed out all night...

*Shit.*

I rose up, a groan beside me. Royal had been so curled up on me he hadn't been prepared for such a quick exit. He pressed palms to his eyes, blinking and looking like Sleeping fucking Beauty's prince. I mean, what the fuck? Who looks that good right when they wake up?

God, I was in so much shit if my dad woke up and I wasn't home.

"Royal, we have to go," I urged, rooting around the blanket for my underwear. "My dad's going to kill me."

"Hmm?" he moaned, looking so stinking cute for such a hard-ass. He also *had* a hard ass, one I had a good view of since I moved the blanket away. He rose up. "What time is it?"

It didn't matter what time it was. It was morning, and I had a curfew. "My dad's seriously going to lose his shit if he realizes I'm not home. He gave me a curfew, and he's frickin' serious about it."

"Okay, okay." He was up now, on his arm and looking at me. Staring for a while, a mischievous gleam in his green eyes, he finally decided to help me when he found my bra.

I ripped it away. "Stop playing around—"

"I'm not, princess." He brought me close, kissing me with a full kiss. He drew me in with firm hands, shutting down my reserve. He grinned against my lips. "I'm just wishing you good morning."

He wished me good morning again when he brought his impressive wingspan around me, and it was Hershey yipping inside the truck to finally make him stop. Even still, he didn't pull away, getting two handfuls of my bare bottom. "Better?" he asked, that gleam back.

Actually, yes. At least temporarily. I smiled a little. "I fucking hate you."

"No, you don't." He flicked my nose. "But we can pretend." Letting me go, he both found and gave me my underwear, finally reaching for his own clothes and getting his own self together after I urged him.

"It's okay, girl. We're leaving," I soothed my dog through the window. Seeing me, Hershey got on her hind legs, wagging her tail. I reached in, giving her a good pet before putting on the rest of my clothes.

140

"It's only six. Maybe you'll be okay." Royal sat on his haunches, bare from the waist up as he gazed at his cell phone with squinting eyes. With the way his jeans slouched low on his hips he definitely didn't have anything on underneath.

*Hot damn.*

My life flashed before my eyes not just due to potential repercussions from my dad, but from my sister who probably wouldn't be too happy to know I screwed her best friend. I probably wouldn't be if it'd been the other way around. I pushed hair out of my face. "We shouldn't have slept together. Paige?"

"It's too late for that now, princess." He pushed his cell phone into his back pocket before reaching down and shrugged his shirt on. He danced blond eyebrows at me. "Don't you think?"

He gave me a kiss after that with another one of his stupidly cute grins. I hadn't found them cute before this morning, more so annoying.

*What the hell is this boy doing to me?*

I knew exactly what he was doing and he did too when he hopped off the truck bed. Landing on boots, he lifted hands for me, twirling me like a damsel before placing me down.

"You're stupid," I told him. "And you're going to get me killed."

"Not if we hurry." He nudged me before going to the driver's side, and as soon as I opened the door, my puppy launched out, making me giggle when she licked my face.

"Don't worry. We're going home—"

I turned upon a rustle in the corn maze, and with the way the breeze moved the long stalks, I actually thought I may have seen something in there. Royal tapped two short honks, making both me and

Hershey freak the fuck out when we jumped. I turned, and he had an arm rested on the wheel, the truck running.

"This chariot ain't going to wait forever, Em," he said, wagging his eyebrows. "Get your ass in here before I change my mind about getting you back."

Why did I have to like it so much when he called me Em?

Groaning, I braced my puppy as I slid inside. Royal went double time back to our cars, but I didn't think it mattered how fast he went. If my dad was up, I was most assuredly dead.

Royal didn't have to follow me home to make sure I got in okay, but since he did, I gave him the job of puppy handler, sliding him keys so he could put Hershey in the guesthouse. If I went inside my dad's house having stayed out all night *and* with living, breathing contraband I was as good as annihilated. His car was in the garage when I pulled in and on quick time, I didn't check to see if Royal got Hershey in the guesthouse okay before going in through the garage. I assumed the best.

"Have you lost your goddamn mind? Staying out all night? What were you thinking?"

Turned out, I should have assumed the worst, peeling my bag off in the house's entryway. My dad was coming down the stairs, his path directly in the line of where the garage door opened to the house.

*Fuck me.*

Dad stepped down a stair, the epitome of rage flashing across his face. "Well? What do you have to say for yourself—"

"She was with me, sir, and I apologize. I lost track of time."

My back shot up, and when I turned, Royal was behind me, sans dog and with my keys in his hands. He followed me through the garage.

*What the hell did he think he was doing?*

"You know how I can be," he said, shocking the hell out of me. He flashed a smile. "We were just hanging out at the pumpkin patch like Paige and I used to."

He had to have a death wish, the only logical explanation he could possibly have for coming into my dad's house and standing up to him. I had visions of shotguns and a wild-eyed father pursing a reckless boy for taking his daughter's honor.

Not an older man who closed his lips.

But that's exactly what my dad did, the man completely silent as Royal stepped into his house and stared at him full on. In fact, the pair stared at each other so long I exchanged a glance between them both, and eventually, Dad worked a hand through his hair.

"I didn't know she was with you," he said, my jaw dropping. *What the fuck?* Dad nodded. "Just don't make a habit of it, all right?"

I seriously felt like I was having an out-of-body experience, Royal standing up to my dad and my dad just taking it like he didn't get off chiding me whenever he had the opportunity. Sometimes, I believed he actually got joy from it he'd done it so much in the past.

"Of course, Mr. Lindquist." Royal's nod was firm. "Definitely won't."

Dad bobbed his head twice in acknowledgment again before closing his robe tight and retreating up the stairs. He went about his business, leaving the pair of us.

"Do you need a ride to school?" Royal asked simply like he didn't just shrink my father down to size. He gave me the keys to the guesthouse. "Hershey's all settled and has breakfast."

My lips parting, I shook my head. "I need to shower and eat."

"Right. Well, I'll see you at school, then." He started to walk off, the front door this time like none of what just happened was a thing at all.

"What was all that about?" I touched his arm, making him turn. "Do you have the magic touch or something when it comes to my dad?" Yeah, he had a history with my dad and Paige being her friend, but that was too weird.

He shrugged. "He's never had a problem with me." I guess not and I released him, but not before he took hold of me. He brought me under one arm, pinching my chin. "I'll see you at school, princess."

He let me go with that, heading to the front door, and all I had left to do then, I guess, was shower.

To: paigealltherage@webmail.com

From: emthegem@webmail.com


Subject: Complications


So something happened with Royal, and I wouldn't be a very good person unless I said something. Actually, I feel like a horrible person and terrible sister. I came down here for you and that's still true, but like I said, something happened, so brace yourself…

I kissed him, okay? All right, I more than kissed him. We hooked up, and before you say what I think you're going to say, this isn't like it was before. Royal isn't Dean, and I don't think he's using me. In fact, he didn't want to do it at all. Neither of us did, and really, because of you. We care about you, but he did this thing at his cousin's pumpkin patch. It was a really sweet thing with some dogs and dog toys, and it made me feel like he wasn't so bad. Of course, that's not the only reason I slept with him. I think he might secretly be a great person, which would explain a lot. It'd explain him and you. He told me about some of the things you used to do and the trouble you got into, and I think I'm starting to understand now. He was your person like you were mine, and I think you might have been his too for him. He said you were there for him, and why am I not surprised? He also told me the reason you left. That girl you mentioned the summer before last? P, why didn't you tell me what was going on? Don't worry. Royal didn't go into details, but I wished you would have. We're here for you, *both* Royal and I, and if you come back, just know you're needed and you're loved. I need you, P, and it's okay to need others and not just be the backbone for me and your friends. It's okay to be weak, and it's okay to be vulnerable as long as you don't let it get you down. You taught me that.

I'm going to do something you asked me to do when you stopped texting and returning my calls over the summer. I've learned a lot since coming here, and the one thing I haven't done for you was the only thing you asked me. You said you needed space, and I never gave that to you. I came here, immersed myself in your life, and became a placeholder for you instead of just being there for you. I'm not going to leave town, but I'm not going to push you either. I'm staying here in Maywood Heights. I'm going to build a life here for now. I don't think it's as bad as you may think…

Let's figure it out together?


Your Forever Love,

Em

Paige >

Sun, Jun 30, 8:27 PM

Any updates? You feel like talking or anything? It's been a while...

Mon, Jul 1, 3:13 PM

Come on, Paige. This isn't cool. I've texted you. Called you. TEXT ME. I'm starting to worry.

Mon, Jul 1, 5:25 PM

Hello? Hello?! Anyone there?

Wed, Jul 3, 1:56 PM

Okay, this is real fucked, Paige, and beyond immature. I called Dad and he said you just took off and didn't come back one night. What's going on? Please TALK TO ME.

Delivered

     Text Message

147

Sun, Jul 14, 9:05 PM

I read over your last text with me. You said to give you space. Well, I've given you that, so please stop with this. I need you...

Wed, Aug 28, 8:19 AM

I'm coming to Maywood Heights, already talked to Dad, Aunt Celeste, and everything. Aunt Celeste doesn't think anything is wrong because you've done this before. Neither does Dad, but I don't care. I'm coming there. I'm coming for you. Be ready.

Delivered

     Text Message

16

Second period English held a study hall, and it'd been the first time I saw Royal since this morning. It'd also been the first time I had really been around Birdie since the fiasco with the dog toys, and I texted her after Mr. Pool left the room for a second.

**Me:** Wanna hang out tonight?

She looked at her phone on her desk, gazing around, and with the room sans teacher, she reached for it.

**Birdie:** Sure. What do you want to do?

I knew that right away, but was I brave enough?

**Me:** I was thinking about going out to Route 80.

Nothing, not even a text message bubble, and I gazed up at her. She had her lip lodged between her teeth, frowning at me before picking up her phone.

**Birdie:** Nuh-uh. No way. That's Court territory.

**Me:** Court territory?

**Birdie:** Yeah, only Court go up there.

**Me:** Why?

**Birdie:** I don't know, but it's off-limits. Want to do something else, I'm game, but going over there... sorry, you're on your own.

She was actually serious, pushed her phone away and everything when she went back to her textbook. What the hell?

**Royal:** Want to hang out tonight? We can go by my place. Watch a movie?

I gazed back at the beautiful boy, his chin rested on his hand as he waited out my response. Everyone else around him was studying, but he was watching me. He flicked up his brow to my phone, and I turned.

*Fuck.*

**Me:** I can't. Sorry, I have other plans.

I turned for his response, but he didn't give much of one. He simply tipped his chin before pulling his book over and studying with everyone else.

*What are you doing?*

I had no idea, but when the bell rang for next classes, I hadn't changed my mind about hanging out with either party, Royal or Birdie. Birdie put her backpack over her shoulder, touching mine, before leaving the classroom. I had no idea what the fuck that meant, so I grabbed my stuff and headed out into the sea after her. I didn't make it far before a heavy arm tossed around my shoulder and a hard body braced me to him.

"I hear we're all hanging out tonight, December," Jax crooned, squeezing me with entirely too much muscle. Soon, I was squished between the likes of him and LJ, Knight bringing up the rear when I turned. I swear he was like the bodyguard, the biggest anyway, and didn't talk much. Jax hugged me. "What are we eating? I'm a fan of pizza. Hey—"

Royal pulled him off me. "She's not hanging out," he said, hitting him with a notebook over the head before easing me into him by the arm. It was a nice warm place to be by his side, and though I had no idea what that meant in regards to us, needless to say I didn't fight him. He leaned in. "And I didn't invite him, by the way, or any of them."

Jax grumbled, the other two grinning before Jax pushed himself between Royal and me. He threw arms around us both. "What's up? You two talking or something?"

"You're warned," Royal growled out. "You got two seconds before…"

"Okay, okay." Jax eased off, and pulling ahead, he walked backwards down the hall. "You don't have to tell me twice. You should come over, though. We all have an awesome time. Like with Paige, we used to—"

"She's not Paige." Royal grabbed his shirt, getting in his face, and all of us stopped in the hall. Everyone in the hall stopped actually, staring at us.

Jax backed down again. "Sorry."

"Yeah." Royal let go, his look apologetic at me, and coming through, LJ parted us to grab Jax. He tugged Jax by the back of his shirt down the hall, LJ shaking his head the whole way.

Royal did too, as well as Knight when he came around. Knight gave Royal and me a nod, letting us go, and with him and all that gone, Royal faced me.

"Got some real hot plans tonight, princess? Have to be if you're turning down an opportunity to hang out with that."

Happy whatever *that* was concluded, I looked at him. "Hardly," I said. Though, I didn't want to lie. "Just got some stuff to do."

"Just got some stuff to do," he parroted, but then smiled. He tugged me closer. "Have fun with that. Invitation is still open if you change your mind, and you're not the new Paige. You're not Paige at all."

I obviously wasn't. I had a feeling he didn't look at Paige the way he was currently looking at me. Not to mention, my sister was an open and proud lesbian, and they were just buddies.

Royal and I weren't buddies.

Actually, I had no idea who the captain of the lacrosse team and I were, but whatever that was had just about everyone in the hallway looking—Mira included. Apparently back, she stared at us across the hallway, looking like she sucked a lemon.

*At least she's alive.*

If that played currently in my favor or not, I didn't know, but in any sense, I was too busy focused on a hot hand presently on my hip. I juggled between that and the sight of the most delicious lips ever having been kissed in recorded history looking hell-bent on taking mine. In the end, Royal didn't, though. He squeezed me once, letting go.

"See you around," he said, and I went the other way, partly to avoid the stares.

The other part was to skip class.

I had no idea how long it would take to get out and explore Route 80, but needless to say, I didn't want to commit to any plans. *Especially* with Royal, who'd most likely be pissed the hell off I even thought about coming out there. Let alone actually going out there, which I did via ride share. I had my driver take me out to the middle of nowheresville, i.e., Route 80. Off the highway and straight into farm country, I traveled back roads with a complete stranger, but I kept my wits about me that the voyage would be worth it. If this was the last place anyone I knew saw my sister, I figured it couldn't hurt to go out there myself and look around. I doubt I'd find anything to help me figure out where she'd gone, but maybe being in that last location would put me in her headspace a little.

At least that's what I told myself.

I felt terrible for lying to Royal and even worse turning down his invitation. He totally wouldn't be on board with me coming out here, though, considering his dad's position, and I didn't want to get him in any hot water for knowing I came out here. I figured coming out during the day while Royal and the other Court boys were in classes would be best. I'd have no witness and could be here as long as I needed. I wasn't opposed to calling Hubert and letting him know I found another ride home that afternoon and mentally prepared for it. I'd go into the night if I had to and see what there was to see.

As it turned out, it wasn't much.

"You sure you want to be left out here, little lady?" my driver asked me, turning around with a frown. "Ain't nothing out here for miles but some train tracks."

Route 80 eventually ended up being a dead end, and I saw both that and the train tracks it intercepted through the window. Still, I needed to get out and take a look myself.

"I'm sure." I paid him, the dude thinking I was completely psycho, no doubt. Since I couldn't anticipate how long I'd be, I didn't want to keep the man waiting for any other rides he could take between my return home. I had reception out here, made sure of it, so I figured I would be okay. After getting out and waving him off, I gripped my book bag and huffed it through overgrown grass. I had to watch my shoes on the blades since I definitely scraped over the occasional broken beer bottle on the way to the rocks leading up to the train tracks.

*Well, now I know what the Court does out here.*

Litter as far as the eye could see, and beer bottles and the butts of both cigarettes and joints lined the rocks. I'd even found some discarded clothing scattered along the way like a boy or two had taken a conquest. I wouldn't be surprised. Clearly, this area was a party spot. That also let me know what Royal and my sister had been doing out here. This was obviously a hangout spot for their crew.

Stepping carefully, I cleared most of the debris, and when I found the train tracks, nothing but farmland surrounded them. I explored. I stayed close to the tracks, scanning the area, and soon, the evidence of trash and social activity fell away. There really was nothing but train tracks, and I walked them after checking out the area around them. I ended up going pretty far before doubling back. I went the opposite way then, and after having traveled for at least a half hour, I stopped.

*Well, this was stupid.*

Clearly, I framed my eyes to combat the sun on a rather surprisingly warm, fall day. Back in town, there'd been a gentle breeze with the colorful trees, but out here, nothing. Deciding to take it easy for a while, I sat on the tracks, just sitting for a while and trying to take it all in. I figured I'd hear or *see* a train pretty easily with nothing out here, so I wasn't shy about leaning back and staring around. After a few moments of that, I put my bag behind me and used it to rest my head on. I didn't know what I was trying to do or accomplish, but decided just being out here was better than nothing.

*Tell me something, Paige.*

Of course, she said nothing, and I closed my eyes, listening for sounds or something. I ended up opening my eyes when a flicker of light escaped through, catching on something between the metal on the tracks. I moved rocks around until I could dig it out.

I held the metal up to the light, the object severally twisted. Putting my finger over divots, I realized there were teeth embedded into the metal.

*A gorilla mouth...*

The thing was a Court ring, damaged to hell but a Court ring nonetheless. Someone must have dropped it out here, and a train went over it at some point. Palming it, I wriggled to get it in my skirt pocket.

"What the hell are you doing out here?"

I rose, but not quick enough because soon, I was off the tracks and being dragged to my feet, a behemoth of a large boy staring into my eyes.

Knight snorted like a bull, and tugging me, he pulled me away from those tracks so fast I barely got a chance to grab my bag. He shook me. "I said, *why* are you here and what in fuck's name are you trying to do?"

I wrestled away, not liking being handled. "How are you out here?" I questioned, ignoring *his* question entirely. "Did you follow me?"

"Fuck yeah, I followed you, and it's a good damn thing I did. I saw you sneaking off campus. It took me a second to get my car, and I lost you a couple times on the way, but once I realized the route you were taking, it was obvious," he grunted. "Why are you here, Lindquist? How do you even know about this place?"

"Royal told me," I said, his eyes widening. "He said it was the last place he saw Paige."

He saw red for some reason, shoving thick fingers into his dark hair. "Fucking hell," he gritted, obviously his favorite choice in curse. He growled. "You're coming with me. *Now*, and leaving this place."

I got the issue Royal's dad had with this place, but frankly, not Knight's. He'd have no reason to be so up in arms unless he was trying to keep Royal out of trouble as well.

Scared all this might get back to his dad someway now, I didn't fight Knight when he led the way to his car. He opened the door for me, pretty much shoving me inside, and after he peeled out and got back on the back roads, the terror inside me grew and grew. Royal's dad obviously figured out that

Royal and some of the guys had been out here. He told Royal that himself, so all of this *could* get back to him. I didn't know how, but it could.

I was in some deep fucking shit.

17

Knight and I got back to a school with bare halls, the time placing us somewhere toward the end of final classes. I made good time considering I believed I'd be out at Route 80 most of the evening, but I doubt Knight would see things that way. He pretty much strong-armed me all the way both into the school and down the hall, and we intercepted, of all people, the headmaster on Knight's way to escort me to my class. He let go of me then, standing back, and Principal Hastings slowly pulled his glasses off his face. He'd been coming out of his office, the King mascot in its fierce growl behind him.

"Mr. Reed," he said, facing Knight before panning to me. He frowned. "Ms. Lindquist. You're both a far cry away from your afternoon classes."

The fact this man knew both our schedules should probably make me feel good my dad was getting his money's worth, but really that kind of freaked me out. We had a lot of students that went to school here.

Principal Hastings approached us. "Explain. Both of you."

Neither of us said anything, Knight bracing his arms as he looked away, and since this was technically my fault for us both being out of classes, I decided to step up.

"They're with me."

I didn't have to when Royal ended up coming down the hallway, his tie loose and jacket off. I noticed he went more and more casual as he went throughout his day, and this wasn't anything new. He frowned at both Knight and me and the situation before shifting his sight to Principal Hastings. Royal slid hands into his pockets. "This is my free period. I asked for their help when I came across a last-minute homecoming crisis."

Principal Hastings's eyebrow rose. "Crisis?"

Royal nodded. "It had to do with the parade timeline, which is due to the homecoming committee at the end of the day. It was an emergency, and they were just headed back to class after we finished up. I realized I still had their hall passes so I followed to make sure they got back okay."

Royal was as cool with his lies as he had been with my dad. So much so that it scared me.

Especially since Principal Hastings backed off.

Returning his glasses to his face, the man nodded, and though he was letting all of us off the hook, he didn't look too keen about it. This also reminded me of my dad, the principal's eyes narrowing at Royal before finding Knight and me.

"Very well," our principal said. "All of you run off. These halls are supposed to be clear between classes."

"Yes, sir," Royal said, always so cool. "I just need two seconds with them first if you don't mind. Some last-minute homecoming stuff. Won't take long."

Honestly, I hadn't even picked up on homecoming or anything of the like since I came to this town, my thoughts solely on my sister. But sure enough, posters and streamers for the upcoming event lined the hallways. This school definitely took all this seriously.

Principal Hastings lowered his head once as he rerouted, going in the opposition direction of us. He stopped just short. "Make it quick the three of you, and, Ms. Lindquist?"

"Uh, yes, sir?"

His eyes narrowed again. "You'd be good to really analyze who you hang out with while attending Windsor Prep," he said, scanning between Knight and Royal. "Wouldn't want you getting into trouble."

His threat felt like less for me and more for Royal and Knight, the latter boy puffing up and getting beside Royal. Principal Hastings gave no mind to that, walking away, and only when he'd cleared the hallway did Royal look at us.

"It was a good thing I was headed to the bathroom; otherwise, you'd both be in some deep shit. What's going on and why did I just do that for both of you?" he asked, then studied me. "Are you all right? Why are you out of class?"

His concern for me and my well-being I couldn't linger on, because with one look from Knight I knew he was about to ruin my entire universe. I saw it in his eyes as he looked at me, his face a grimace.

"I followed your girl to Route 80," he said, Royal ripping his gaze away and flashing it on Knight. Knight frowned. "That's right. Followed her right off campus. She took a ride share out there, and told me you told her that's the last place you saw Paige."

"I did tell her that," he said, deadpan when he said it, but his expression was regretful. In actuality, he looked like he'd been taken for a ride, and no one gave him the courtesy of a sick bag, his jaw working as Knight backed away from us.

"I'm going to class," Knight said, his hands up. "Handle that."

*Handle that.* Like I needed to be handled...

Maybe I did. I clearly overstepped on something I didn't understand here, something that made the boy who looked at me so differently in recent hours reverse any work he'd done to get there. The anger crept up his neck in deep red tones, his strong jaw piercing as tight as his temple.

I thought to speak so he wouldn't have to first.

"Royal, let me explain," I said. He raised his hands, but I kept on. "Remember how you told me you went out to Route 80 because of Paige, to be at the last place you guys were at together? Well, that's kind of why I went there too. I thought maybe being in the last place you saw her might get me in her headspace a little. I might figure out where she may have gone."

Hearing it out loud now sounded incredibly stupid. Even to me, the one with the so-called plan and the information did nothing to help.

Royal shut down completely during my word vomit, looking pained even, and I cringed.

"I know I wasn't supposed to go out there," I rushed. "I know that, and I know your dad didn't want anyone out there, Royal, but I had to go. I had to. You have to understand."

Narrowed eyes flicked my way. "I didn't tell you that information so you could go around and do whatever the fuck you wanted with it."

"I know that. I know—"

"No, you don't know," he said, lifting a hand. "You couldn't possibly know. You know nothing about my dad, this... town, and you know nothing about me."

*Ouch.* "Well, let me try, then."

"Why should I?" he asked, digging the dagger deeper. The red crept further up his neck. "I can't trust you."

My insides caved, a balloon bursting inside my chest and making me feel empty and hollow. I grabbed his arm. "Royal—"

He pushed my hands away. "I'm done with all this."

He walked away down the empty hall, shoving his hands into his pockets, as he watched his own steps down the hall. He did so in deep concentration and very much *without* me.

18

That next few days at Maywood Heights felt as cold as the first, the only difference was no one spoke to me. No one looked at me... It was like a silent summons had been cast over the entire place, and even the teachers barely made eye contact with me. I had to raise my hand if I wanted to be addressed at all, and the same went with Birdie and the rest of our friends. They went to classes with me, let me eat with them, but any responses to me were one or two words and the conversations were well outside of me. They kept them focused on the upcoming basketball season, other things that went on before I arrived in town. They *shut me out*, and at first, I thought it'd been in my head. After my showdown with Royal in the hall, I figured I'd "othered" myself on purpose. I'd felt so damn guilty for what I had done and the clear betrayal of his trust that at first I only gave one- or two-word answers to questions. I didn't raise my hand and avoided eye contact, but as I came out of my shell, there was a clear blackballing going on here. I didn't understand it.

Until I did.

I caught the Court looking at me one day from their lunch table, LJ, Jax, and Knight and everyone else. They all looked at me in one conjoined effort, but the only one who'd been too busy was Royal. He chewed a sandwich, paying attention to nothing but his food, and the staredown made me lose all appetite for mine. I picked up my stuff, excusing myself from Birdie and the others, and dumped my tray. What was worse was I was barely acknowledged at all when I got up. Only when I went to the lunchroom doors and faced back at that center table did anyone notice I left.

The Court had a warning in their eyes before they headed back to their conversations, and that couldn't be denied. They were telling me to tread lightly.

They were telling me to stay away.

I'd been naive about the power within this place, the almighty Court ruled the school, but I hadn't been on the receiving end of it. I only saw that power thrust upon teachers, other students, the headmaster, and even my own dad. These people were threatened by eighteen-year-old boys and a club/society way older in this town than me.

"Have a good evening, Ms. Lindquist."

I did still have Hubert, the older man staring at the rearview mirror when I let myself out to go inside the house. I didn't have to work tonight, thank God, and called in sick after the one shift I had these past few days. I realized very quickly during that shift I wasn't welcome there either. LJ, though he talked to me, had me scrubbing down that whole place with basically a toothbrush he called a scrubber, and he stayed with me too, stood over me like slave labor. He watched me scrub, and when he didn't like *the way* I scrubbed, he made me do it again. The cherry to the night was coming outside and seeing him, Jax, and Knight and some other boys in the Court at their cars, Royal with them. Royal had been with Mira, just talking, and though he didn't have his arm around her or anything, it still hurt seeing them together. Needless to say, I rushed into my car, not that he actually looked at me or anything. He didn't at school, and he hadn't then.

I dragged my feet up the stairs and into the house, my only saving grace out back, who I immediately went to tend to after I hung up my bag and took my uniform jacket off. Hershey continued to basically double in size, and though I probably should check around for my dad, I needed to see her so bad today. It was another lonely day at Windsor Prep, and I immediately went for the one thing who would ease that. Taking my key out, I unlocked the door to the guesthouse.

The kibble… was everywhere, like she'd turned over her dish and left it scattered, but not just that. The sheets on the guest bed were tattered, the pillows tossed as if she'd had a fit or something and her box was crushed, a shoe print right in the center of it.

*A shoe print.*

"Rosanna, Rosanna!" I screamed once inside the main house. I ran both upstairs and down, freaking out through the whole house. "Rosanna, it's Hershey. She's gone. She's—"

"You won't find her."

My dad's voice came from his office, a place in the house I never ventured through. I never had a reason. It was his space.

He looked up at me as I backed up, getting into his vantage point. He sat at a wide desk, going over papers.

I dampened my lips. "Where is she?"

"I fired her," he said, completely dismissive about it. He bowed his head, writing. "Fired her for allowing you to bring an animal into this house and helping you harbor it." He gazed up with a frown. "Really, December. What were you think?"

My world literally crumbed around me by what he was saying, Rosanna… Hershey.

"Dad, I…"

"You what?" He folded his hands. "What could you possibly say when you've been lying to me for God knows how long about a damn dog—"

"Her name's Hershey."

I cut him off and his eyes twitch wide, borderline madness within them.

His jaw ticked. "I don't care what its name is."

"Well, you should care," I challenged, making him blink. "You should care about me, and that dog is the only real kind of anything I've had since I've been here. From you or anything else."

"You have food from me, *stuff*, and education. Not to mention a roof over your head." He curled fingers in his hair. "What more do you want from me?"

If he had to ask, he'd never know. Being a parent wasn't just taking care of me physically. One would think he'd learn that since his eldest ran out on him.

"Where are you going?" Dad came around his desk, but I was already leaving, heading to the kitchen where I grabbed keys. "December—"

"I'm going to get my dog, and I don't care if I have to tear up this city to find her."

"She's been taken by animal control, but you won't bring her back to this house," he said, coming around the bar. "You saw what that animal did to my guesthouse."

I did see, the evidence of a frightened dog being taken by people she didn't know or trust. My throat thick, I shook my head at him. "Bye, Dad."

"I'm warning you, December. You leave this house and bring that dog back, you might as well not come home."

The words chilled me, but they didn't stop me. I went out to the garage, got in my sister's car, then pulled out. I was going to have my puppy with me when I came back.

I guess I just wouldn't come back here.

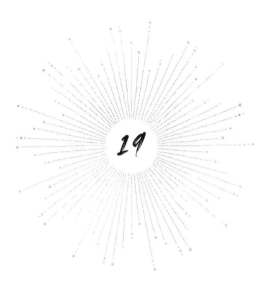

## 19

"A chocolate Labrador puppy? Yeah, we acquired one of those, but she's been moved to the veterinary clinic on third. Let me give you the address."

The fear Hershey had to be moved to a vet clinic caused me to hit the gas faster. The woman on the phone couldn't tell me why she'd been moved from the local pound, but just that she had and that was enough for me to move in quick time. I pulled up to the vet clinic just after dark and barely closed the door before rushing up to a building that was completely pitch black outside of the front building lights.

"Hello, hello!" I tapped on the glass and to my relief someone was in there. The lights flickered on, and a woman in scrubs came down the hall.

She opened the door. "Can I help you, miss?"

I explained the situation with mush mouth. I mean, completely incoherent, and I even shed a few tears. I couldn't help it. Hershey was my friend and I needed her back, and though the woman sympathized, she shook her head.

"I'm sorry," she said, sighing. "I don't know why the puppy was brought in, but I can't just give her to you. She was brought in today by the vet himself, and he must have had a reason."

"Can we look at her? If you can see if there's nothing wrong, can I take her?"

She shook her head again. "I'm not a vet, miss."

"Please, please, please. You don't understand. She's mine, and if she is hurt… if she's scared, she needs me, *please*."

Her hands held the door, so much debate on her face, and I prayed for small favors. This woman had no reason to let me inside this building right now.

But for whatever reason, she did.

She waved me in, locking the door quickly, and I followed her through intricate halls to the back. The place was really nice. In fact, I'd venture to say top notch for a vet clinic. I was used to seeing run-down places where I was from, but the white walls and shining tiles were completely opposite of that. The whole place was elite and not much unlike everything else around this town I'd come to find myself immersed in. The clinic was shiny and polished like anything else, and in the back were cages. They were all empty.

All except for one.

I rushed over, Hershey… my silly little puppy up on her hind legs and waging her tail at me. She looked completely okay. If anything, more than, and when the woman saw us together she laughed a little, shaking her head.

"I guess she knows her mama," she said, opening the cage for me. Hershey didn't even let the woman pull her body out before bounding over her and into my arms.

I caught her easily, giggling through tears, and I thought I lost my damn mind. I was crying over a dog, but she wasn't just a dog. She was mine, my friend.

"Hey, honey girl," I crooned, cradling her. "You okay?"

"Appears that way." The woman gazed at a chart on the cage, scanning it. "The doctor did a full workup on her today, and she's fine. She's actually queued to be released."

"So I can take her?" I asked, hope in my voice. "You see she's mine. We're each other's."

She smiled at that, but then chewed her lip a little. "I'll tell you what. I'll give her to you, but I will need to get your personal information before you leave. I'm only doing this because Dr. Anderson does bring strays in from time to time, and when he does, they usually go to a no-kill shelter for adoption. It's only because of that, and *only that*, I'm letting you have her. Adoption doesn't seem to be needed for this little one."

She rubbed Hershey's head beside me, and the ham Hershey was leaned right into it. I petted her for a while before the woman came over with a personal information chart for me to fill out.

"Go ahead and fill this out and please don't lie," she said. "I'm going to call your cell phone to make sure it's correct before you leave."

They really didn't want animals going out to the wrong hands, and though I appreciated that, it made me nervous I did have to lie about my address. I obviously couldn't go home to my dad and had a feeling I'd be sleeping in my sister's car tonight. I wouldn't be calling Birdie or anyone, not with how they'd barely been talking to me.

Hershey in hand, I took a pen to the paper, starting with my name and the other easy stuff. The woman watched me for a while before saying she'd come back.

"I've got to finish my rounds," she said. "I was cleaning before locking up for the night. I gotta take the trash out, but I'll be right back."

I nodded, watching her go before going back to the paperwork. I could leave right now with Hershey in hand, but she'd done me a solid, so I didn't want to do that. Hershey licked my ear, and I dropped my pen.

"You want to get out of here? Huh?" I teased, laughing before going down to the floor to find it. I found the pen quickly, but on the way up, I froze.

Smoke… billowing smoke curled across the floor in a waft, and standing, I noticed it eased out from behind the door the woman left through.

*What the hell?*

I ran toward the door, touching it with the back of my hand and a sharp burn pulled me back.

My shoes blended with smoke, flames through opaque glass on the other side, and panicking, I braced Hershey and rerouted for another door. I touched it with the back of my hand again, and when it came up cold, I went for the knob.

I ran out into smoky halls, covering my face and trying to remember how I got into this place. There'd been too many twisting turns, those squeaky white floors now covered in smoke, and I ventured into it.

174

Hershey whined, then barked as I choked upon inhalation. A crash sounded when a shelf or something burst through window glass next to me, making me scream and fall to my knees. Flames from above beat through the window, and Hershey yelped, wrestling from my arms and escaping down the hall.

"Hershey!"

She ran into smoke the opposite way of the fire, and I crawled on my elbows, attempting to scurry after her. The flames from above chased me down the hall, and I stayed low, attempting to avoid them.

They were everywhere, creeping and eating the walls like a flesh-eating disease and I backed up on the floor, the horror of it all sinking me into the depths. I had strong fears I'd die in this place, that *Hershey* would die and I wouldn't be able to find her. The latter thought alone got me back on my feet and running out of the hall engulfed in flames. I found another door and pushed myself through it.

Only to find myself against a hard chest.

Unyielding rock literally slammed into me, strong hands as they pulled me and forced me to gaze up into dazzling green eyes.

"December, what the fuck?" Royal gritted out, his eyes wild. "What are you doing here? We need to get you out of here. Let's go, now!"

Why was *he* here? I had no time to ask as he was quite literally picking me up and forcing me out of the place. I kicked, screaming about Hershey, but he ignored me. Too hell-bent to get me out. Eventually, we surfaced to clear air on the outside, but as soon as my feet hit the ground, I was running right back to the building.

He dragged me back before I could get too far, and when he braced my shoulders, he shook me. "Are you goddamn crazy? What are you doing?"

"Hershey's in there," I choked, smoke still in my lungs. I reached toward the building. "Hershey, Hershey!"

I fought him, wild with all remaining strength I had, but like before, he overpowered me. He forced me to sit on the ground, and before I knew it, he was pulling the collar of his dress shirt up, covering his face and rushing into the building himself.

"Royal!"

*He* had to be damn crazy now to rush into a burning building, save me, then rush right back to save my dog. I sat in crippling fear on my bottom while sirens sounded in the distance around me. Help was coming, but I didn't know how fast.

Getting to my feet, I considering going in again.

But then, a miracle.

A barking dog was in a boy's arms, a boy who had dirt and soot all over his handsome face and school uniform. The door they came through burst out in flames following their exit, and though Royal almost dropped my dog, he didn't. He held her tight, coming to me while gasping for air, but he never once let go of Hershey.

"You're damn crazy," he said, falling to his knees while he hacked, but with a few licks from Hershey on his dirty face, he smiled a little. "Both of you are."

Placing her down, he petted her once before gripping his knees to collect himself. She went immediately to me, and I hugged her, trying to figure out what the fuck just happened. My eyes widened at a realization. "There was a woman in here with me. Is she okay—"

"She's who let me in," he said, waving off my panic. "And called the fire department after we both saw smoke. We both got out, but when she told me a girl was in there, I went back in. I had no idea it'd be you."

I braced Hershey, glad the woman was okay, but…

"Why are you here?" I asked, those sirens coming closer. "Did you know about Hershey being here?"

"Yes," he said, making my insides clench. He knew…

And then a thought hit me, a harsh thought that couldn't be. He was one of only a handful of people who knew about Hershey, and on top of that, he was mad at me at the present.

My jaw moved. "Did you tell?"

His eyes flickered my way following another cough. "What?"

"Did you tell my dad about Hershey?" Any heroism he may have shown I threw out the window at the possibility, and such an act seemed just dark enough he'd actually do it. He'd been right that day in the hall when he let into me. I didn't know him.

Royal got to his back, coughing as he shook his head. "Of course I didn't. The reason I'm here is for her. *I'm* why she's here and not at a pound."

None of that made sense. How would he know Hershey was even at the pound to get?

"Mira," he let me in on. "She gave your dad an anonymous tip at his office. I guess she saw us that night at the pumpkin patch. Her dad's the other owner, and though she doesn't live on the property, she happened to be there that night. Fuck, she probably watched us the whole goddamn night."

The disgust of that I ignored for the red I saw. "She told?"

"Yeah, caught her bragging about it to some of the cheerleaders." He rose up, dangling muscular arms over his knees. "After I heard, I called around, and when I figured out where Hershey was, I had my uncle come and get her. This is his vet clinic. I was coming to get her now to take her to Windsor House. I figured, better than the damn pound."

"Why?" My throat was thick again, tight. "Why would you do that?" He'd been ignoring me, made *others* ignore.

He faced me. "Because I'm putting my neck out for you for some reason. Because I *keep* putting my neck out for you, fuck." He forced fingers through sooty blond hair. "It's like I'm a goddamn glutton for punishment or something, helping you out as some sick way to do right by Paige and take care of her sister while she's gone or something…"

He'd ranted, that I knew.

But that didn't stop the fact that he said it.

Royal Prinze had spoken his truth, and I'd been completely there for it.

I dampened my lips. "So was screwing me looking out for me too?"

Royal's eyes flashed like he just realized, like everything he said he was suddenly there for too. "December…"

"No, it's fine."

"December. Em—"

He grabbed my arm, but I pulled away.

"You don't call me that," I said, shaking my head. "Only my sister calls me that."

His lids lowered. "December, let me…"

"No," I gritted and reaching into my pocket, I took out the ring I found on the tracks. I threw it at him, and of course, he caught it easy. My jaw worked. "I found that on the tracks that day at Route 80. It's evidence I'm not the only one who thinks you and your Court are a bunch of assholes."

He said nothing as he'd been lifting up the ring, and by that time, the fire trucks and EMTs had finally come. The building burst into flames behind us, a manifested end to the fucked-up-ness that was my start with Royal Prinze.

20

Royal decided to opt out of going to the hospital after getting checked out by the EMTs. He'd been deemed fine and had no reason to stay, so he didn't. He left so quick, in fact, I hadn't seen him leave, and just as well. He was the last person I wanted to see right now, and though I'd been told I was fine too, I did decide to go to the hospital. It'd give me more time to figure out what I should do now that I was homeless and with a little dog. I'd also been told they'd have someone come to the hospital to check Hershey out since I inquired, and I wanted to make sure she was good too. They let us ride in the back of the ambulance and everything, but any thrill that might have come from that burst into fiery flame just like the vet clinic that burned when we ventured away from it. I had no idea what'd been up with the fire or how it happened, but it sure did expose a lot of bullshit. I wanted to leave it and everything about this place behind, and now that I had Hershey back, there was really no reason to stay.

I dangled my feet for a long time as I sat on a white hospital bed, my arm covered in a white bandage. I'd caught an ember or something trying to escape the fire, and the doctor here wanted more of a look at the work the EMTs did on me. While I waited, my puppy currently had the time of her life in the children's ward of the hospital. She'd also been given a clean bill of health by a local vet they brought in. The only reason she wasn't here now was because the nurse wanted to show her around to some of the kids who *wouldn't* be getting out of here tonight for various ailments. It gave Hershey something to do and me a minute's ease to get my head together. I basically had no choice but to go back to my aunt after this. She'd been called and gave me an earful for running into that building after a dog. She was happy I was okay, though, and after I begged to go home, she said she'd look into getting Hershey and me a flight. Aunt Celeste had several dogs growing up, so she said the new addition would be okay. She just wanted to make sure I was sure about coming home.

I hoped I was.

After the doctor gave me the all clear, he stepped out for a second, and that's when half the basketball team came into the room, Birdie ahead of them. Several nurses attempted to fight them all back, but Birdie was able to make her way through as the staff said, "One at a time." It turned out she was that one, and after waving off the team, Shakira and Kiki amongst them, Birdie joined me near the examination table, nothing but a wild panic on her face.

"Holy hell, girl," she said, noticing my arm immediately. It looked worse than it actually was, a first-degree burn. "Shit. It's true. You and Royal were in a fire? What the hell?"

"How did you find out?" I asked, actually happy to see her despite how she and the others had been ignoring me. I guess I couldn't help but long for friendship in a time of vulnerability.

"The news," she said, looking up from the bandage to my eyes. "You two are all over it."

I forgot they'd been there, asking questions I didn't want or know how to answer about the fire and ones Royal had flat-out refused to answer. He'd been on the other side of the lot, but I'd watched as he held a hand up and washed his hands of the media. He'd zoomed away in his Audi quickly after that, nothing more than a bandage to secure a cut on his forehead, and his thoughts definitely hadn't been on me. He'd left without checking to see if I was okay.

Again, all as well.

I owed him nothing, and he owed me nothing.

"You okay?" she asked, frowning. "That looks pretty gnarly."

It really did look worse than it was. I shook my head. "I'll be fine. Just a small burn. The doctor is actually getting my final paperwork now so I can leave."

Her head bobbed twice, that big fluffy ponytail always on her head. She gazed at the table, and I moved so she could sit.

She folded her hands. "Is it true you ran into a building after a dog? That Royal did too and saved it and you?"

If information and hot gossip were the only reason she was here, she could go somewhere. I frowned. "Is that why you're here?"

"No," she said, lowering her head. "I'm here because I've been a shit friend."

That much was for sure. She'd abandoned me just because Royal, and most likely the others, wanted her to. One crossed him and the Court, and one put a mark on themselves, a mark she clearly didn't feel I was worth branding.

"I'm sorry, December." She lifted her head, breathing hard. "This is just a fucked situation."

"What happened?" I asked, really not knowing the details or anything. "Did Royal ask you not to talk to me or…"

"No, it wasn't like that. He didn't ask anyone not to talk to you, but there were rumors going around that you two got into it." She sighed. "The Court can ruin lives. I guess we all went chicken shit, but it was dumb. The Court and Royal Prinze don't rule me, and Shakira, Kiki, and the other girls feel the same."

Still, I wouldn't want them to ruin their lives over me. Especially since I planned to leave.

"I get it." I did. Royal scared me quite a few times, the power he had over the school and even the *adults* in this town. The only person who seemed to elicit any type of fear in him had been his dad, and that completely made sense—the man was scary, and I wouldn't want to cross him. Everyone else basically bowed down to Royal. Well, everyone but me. I did stand up to him.

*"I keep putting my neck out for you…"*

I swallowed. "Are people saying anything about us?"

Birdie frowned. "There are some rumors, yeah. Mira saying stuff. Saying she saw you two and…"

So now, I was a whore. All of this was so close to home and what happened in LA before I came here it was scary, but I wasn't about to have a repeat of all that.

"I'm going home," I told her, making her eyes widen. "I thought coming here might convince my sister to come back. I was stupid."

"Don't go because of all this. Me? December, I'm so sorry for what happened, and Mira is a complete bitch. You'd give her exactly what she wants by running off."

I sighed. "I don't really have anywhere to go, B. My dad kicked me out tonight. It was actually about the dog Royal saved. My dad doesn't want one in his house, and…" I shook my head. "I have nowhere else to go."

"That's not true."

I panned, my eyes widening at the presence of my father. He'd been called too, along with my aunt, actually the first to be called, but they hadn't been able to reach him. I figured he'd been busy, or rather didn't care. He'd shown similar lack of care before.

He was here now, his sport coat on and his hands in his pockets. He gazed at my arm with a stern look on his face, and my heart sunk. I was in for a second round of what started tonight.

"I'm going to wait outside, okay?" Birdie stated, squeezing my shoulder before allowing my dad in. She acknowledged him with a nod, and then he was standing before me.

I slid off the table. "Dad?"

Why would he even bother coming? He spoke his position before. He said if I came back with a dog, I might as well not come back, the complete opposite of what he'd just said.

He approached. "The hospital just got to me. I saw the rest on the news. You went into the building after that dog? December, what were you thinking?"

See… more of this, and I wasn't taking it. I touched my bandage. "You don't have to worry. Aunt Celeste is getting me a flight back to LA. You won't have to deal with me anymore. Just like Paige."

I watched that flash across his eyes, and sliding his hands out of his pockets, he sighed.

"I don't want you to feel that way," he said, surprising me. "And I don't want you to think that I feel that way about you or Paige."

How were we supposed to feel? He'd *always* been that way, to both of us after Mom died. He may have been hurting, lashed out at us, but we were hurting too and needed him. We needed *our dad*, not all this judgment he constantly threw at us.

"I'm disappointed by what you did tonight," he continued. "But I'd be remiss in saying I didn't have anything to do with it."

Surprised again, I found his eyes, the man nodding as if to confirm to me what had been said.

His jaw moved. "You ran after that dog because of me and you went into that building because of me, and I own that. I suppose my initial reaction was because of your lies and not the dog itself."

"I didn't want to lie," I said, the truth. I felt I had to because I could never talk to him.

He acknowledged that, lowering his head. "And I feel like you're being honest about that. I don't make it easy. I know that."

He'd said the words towards the window, anywhere but me. This was all hard for him, that I knew, and it was hard for me too. This was probably the longest conversation I had with my dad in a long time. Probably since before Mom died, and we were all a family with Paige.

He dampened his lips. "I didn't do well with your sister. I gave up on her, and I'd like not to do that with you too."

Out of his pocket came something pink, something with a silver bell and a name tag. It was a collar, the name "Hershey" clearly written into a bone-shaped dog tag.

"The damn pet store had no reception," he said, handing the collar out to me. "I would have been here sooner if I'd gotten the hospital's calls. Your dog's Hershey, right? Like the candy bar."

I took the collar, not knowing what to say. I swallowed. "Yeah, that's right."

It was so pretty, *thoughtful*, and nothing like my dad.

He turned his hands to his pockets. "Now, there will be rules with this. There are places in the house she won't be able to go. You'll keep her mostly in your room and in the house common areas."

Completely okay with that, I told him so, my heart squeezing. "I promise," I said to emphasize I would.

He smiled, just slight but he did. "And I expect you to clean up after her, take her out and feed and water her. That won't be Rosanna's job…"

"Rosanna?" I asked.

"Yes, I hired her back after you ran off, and with a handsome raise for the inconvenience. I was angry at you and took it out on her, and I apologized. She's gratefully agreed to come back, but she won't be cleaning up after that dog—"

"She won't." I shook my head. "She won't. I'll do everything. Hershey's with one of the nurses. They said I could get her after I got checked out."

"All right, then," he said. "We should probably go see what's up with that, then head home. The doctors tell me you're okay. I'm glad."

He actually meant that, and for the first time, I believed it. I had no idea what was happening here, but after my dad told me he'd go see what was up with the doctors so I could check out, I didn't care. I just wanted to stay.

I wanted to try if he did too.

## 21

I had to give it to Mira. She made sure word traveled fast about Royal and me, and what that meant for my reputation at Windsor Prep Academy equated to something similar to what I'd already gone through. I left a lot of bullshit back in my old life, and coming here, starting anew where no one knew me, that had been the one relief about starting over. No one did know me. No one knew my *past*, and I thought I left that life back in LA. It all came back with Mira's not-so-tall tales about Royal and me at McAlester's Pumpkin Patch, but the difference was I didn't regret what happened between Royal and me. I didn't own up to it since it was no one's business, but I wasn't ashamed I'd done it. I'd wanted to be with him that night because I'd trusted him. He hadn't gone out there with certain intentions. Us being together just happened, and because of that, the rumors that followed me now didn't break me. They didn't roll off my back by any means, but their foundations were different. Therefore, the way I handled them was different.

It only helped that I had friends who actually stuck by me this time rather than run away with the rumor mill. Birdie and the rest of the basketball team hung in there with me. They *stood up* for me when everyone else either whispered around me or stopped talking completely when I walked into the room. They didn't stop talking to me and hassled anyone who did. I had Amazon-sized women acting as a force around me, and I had to say, it felt pretty damn good.

The days in Maywood Heights started to feel good. At least when it came to everything but Royal. He was still around, and I saw him, but we didn't talk to each other. We were like passing ships, a lot of words whispered around us, but none of them shared between us. He actually missed quite a few days of school after the fire, the thing deemed a freak accident in the end. It turned out the fire had been completely electrical, and from what I understood, Royal was fine but had been missing classes for some reason. I saw him more in the days leading up to homecoming. He'd been at the pep rallies and, of course, at the parade with the rest of the Court jocks. He rode on the lacrosse float while I stood at the sidelines. He looked at me then, looked at me long with a bare chest covered in spirit paint and a face sectioned off in the tones of navy and orange. So many unspoken words were between us.

At least on my part.

I opted out of the homecoming dance itself. Besides the fact that no one asked me (oddly enough, being the girl Royal Prinze slept with left me pretty lonely when it came to dates), I'd been focusing more on school and home life. I tried to be home when my dad got in, just trying to be around, and I noticed he did too. He didn't work late for the most part, and his weekend trips and social events were few and far between. He was trying too, and though he wouldn't admit it, I caught him tolerating Hershey quite a few times. When she nipped as his leg, he didn't stop her. He even fed her some of his breakfast in the morning instead of toeing her away. He was learning to live with me and a dog, and we were learning to do the same.

**Birdie:** I can't believe you're not going to the dance tonight! I'm going to feel so bad about posting everything online with you at home. :(

I'd gone shopping with Birdie and the other girls for the dance and everything and assured them then that me not being there was fine. They could post all they wanted. No FOMO, or "fear of missing out," would be made in my neck of the woods.

**Me:** You know it's cool. Have fun.

I had every intention of spending homecoming night with Hershey, me, and a box of pizza. We'd probably take a walk too since, at some point, we wouldn't have too many more of these nice fall days before the winter hit. This wasn't like California.

I scratched behind her ears while she burrowed in my bedding, about to call for that pizza when Rosanna called me downstairs.

"You got someone here to see you, December," she said somewhere in the house, and I picked up Hershey, putting her in her own cute dog bed *Dad* had bought for her. He could say what he wanted, but he was starting to like this dog. He came home with stuff for her every once in a while, this bed being one of the gifts.

I smiled at her, watching as she played on her own before heading downstairs. I passed Rosanna at the foot of the stairs along the way, the woman wiping down a dish with a coy smile.

"Living room," she said, walking away, and I eyed her as she made her way down the hall and to the kitchen. Yep, I had no idea what that was about, but then, I made my way to the living room and quickly found out.

Royal Prinze stood in a tux, patent leather shoes on his feet and a white orchid on his lapel. The tiny flower was made completely out of paper and just as lovely as he was, the boy clean-shaven and his hair perfect and pushed back.

I stepped into the room, his tux hitting him at all magnificent angles. He made me feel ordinary in our school uniforms, but here and like this now, I was very much a peasant before an actual prince. My lips parted. "What are you doing here?"

The captain of the lacrosse team was in my living room, rocking his homecoming best, and not at homecoming, so yes, this required some explanation. For whatever reason, him being here didn't surprise him, the boy coming forward. He had his hands behind his back, his shoulders big and strong.

"Wanted to see why you aren't going to homecoming," he said simply, frowning. He lifted a shoulder. "And maybe offer you an alternative."

Too many things were going on in this room, too many words when before he had none either for me or to me. I decided to leave the latter part of what he said, focusing on the first.

"How did you know I wasn't going?" Only Birdie and my friends knew.

"Besides the fact that you're not in any of Birdie's photos she's posted," he started, closing more distance. "I hadn't heard anyone ask you."

No one had asked me, not him either...

At least until now.

He eased a hand into his pocket, and when it came out, he showed me the most dazzling orchid. It was green like his eyes and matched his vest and tie. It was also paper, and after fluffing the thing up, he held the tiny flower in his large hand.

"I said a lot of things I didn't mean the night of the fire," he said, all of that moving so harshly on his face. "Things I regret. I won't lie to you. Yes, it did start that way. You're my best friend's sister, so yeah, that's how it was."

It made sense, I guess. I was his best friend's sibling so he had my back, but I never asked him to do that.

"What changed?" I asked, my breath leaving as he took my wrist and slid that pretty orchid over my wrist. I idly wondered if he made it himself, made it for me, but with his smile, I forgot all that. As stated before, he didn't do it a lot, but each and every time, it'd been in my presence. It'd been around me.

His long fingers moved under the ribbon tied to the orchid, his eyes on me. "Knowing you," he said simply. "And really that's it."

That was it, wasn't it? And I'd be lying myself if I also hadn't gone in with certain thoughts about him. Those changed too. *I* changed my mind too about him.

He laced our fingers together, stalling my breath again, and when that grin of his widened, he made my tummy jump even more.

"I guess I have to admit something else since I'm putting it all out on the floor now," he said, bringing me close. "I might have had something to do with why you weren't asked to homecoming. Actually, I totally am."

My jaw dropped. "Did you threaten people?"

"Knight may have," he said, those bright eyes dancing a little. "Then Jax and LJ…"

"What the fuck, Royal—"

He grabbed me, pulling me into a hard chest, and I melted.

Especially when he touched our foreheads together.

His breath was so warm, his fingers brushing my chin. "You're not going with someone else because I was stupid. Because I couldn't fucking talk to you and say sorry, which I am."

I'd been stupid too, but I wouldn't be now, and when he tipped my chin up, I let him move his lips into mine. I let him taste my tongue, and I let him fold me into his big arms. This boy was so, so dangerous for me. He was as harsh and raw as he was addictive and sometimes even cruel, but for whatever reason, I kept coming back. I kept stepping into the danger.

I kept folding into the heat.

"I don't have a dress," I said, pulling away a little, and we both stepped back at the sudden presence of another. Rosanna had apparently been watching us. Maybe not the whole time because, when she came into the room, she had something in her arms.

The dress was white, long, and covered in shimmering rhinestones and pearls. It was so fancy and something completely different from what I normally wore.

She smiled a little. "I snuck this into the back of your sister's closest, hoping one day she'd wear it," she said, bringing it over and lining it up with my body. "So how about you warm it up until she comes back?"

## 22

I wore the dress with my nose ring, and even if it was against the school's dress code, I didn't care tonight. That was the one little piece of me, and I was going to lean into it. It went friggin' awesome with the dress as well as Royal's orchid perfectly. I came downstairs completely me, my new self and my old self combined, and Royal was there to receive me at the foot of the stairs. He'd been waiting in the foyer, and looking all hot and stuff, I truly did feel like a princess. Especially with the look he gave me as I came down. He waited like Prince Charming, his large chest rising and falling like he was trying to catch his breath. Dare I say, Royal Prinze was at a loss for words.

"I love it," he said, mentioning my nose when he tapped his. Something about that put me more on a high than I already was. He took my hand next, kissing it, and Rosanna got about a thousand pictures for my dad, who wasn't off work yet. He normally would be, but I told him I wasn't going to the dance, and he figured I might want the night to myself to watch TV and do girly things. He'd actually said that, *my dad*.

I laughed a little at the thought, posing for one last picture for Rosanna before she sent us off. She closed the door, and after, Royal took my hand.

"I have to admit just one more thing," he said, taking me down the stairs. "I'm not technically asking you to the dance tonight... at least not alone."

"It's about damn time."

The boys came out of a limo parked by the curb one by one, LJ, Jax, and Knight all in tuxes with varying fits, heights, and colors. All wore orchids matching their vests, but none wore green. That was only Royal and me.

Jax, the one who spoke, sprinted up to us, throwing an arm around Royal, which looked pretty fucking funny considering their height difference. Royal had about half a foot on him, elbowing him to let him go, and after mocking hurt on his face, Jax held an arm out to me.

"Mademoiselle," he said, bowing. He grinned. "And might I say, you look lovely tonight. You're totally rocking that nose jewelry."

He said it with a wink, and I laughed. I eyed the arm he gave but, in the end, took it. "What's going on?"

"We're your dates," Jax crooned, wagging his eyebrows. He placed a hand on mine. "Which I have to say is a pretty fucking big deal. We don't take girls to dances. We dance with them, but we don't take them. Keeps our options open, ya know?"

I chuckled, taking LJ's arm too when he put it out. "So why the exception for me, then?"

"Because you're not just a girl," LJ said, smiling when the limo door opened for me. It'd been Knight to do it, his own smile light. LJ leaned in. "You're family."

My lips parted at that, a hand resting on my back. I didn't have to turn to know it was Royal. He guided me inside, and his lot surrounded behind us in the back. Before we took off, Jax opened the limo top and stood out of it.

"Get us going, good sir," Jax said to the driver, tapping the top. "We got a dance to attend."

Showing up with not one but *four* dates to the Windsor Prep Academy dance would have been something, but the fact that my dates were Royal and three other boys in the Court... let's just say we got a few eyes. A few of which were Mira and her friends. They'd been by the punch bowl with their own dates, non-Court guys surprisingly. Maybe that had been Royal's doing, maybe not, but for whatever reason, she wasn't being escorted by Windsor Prep royalty tonight, *I was.*

"Hey, Mira," I said, passing her on Knight's arm at the time. She made me out to be a ho to pretty much everyone in this room, but at the moment, I didn't care. I was sitting pretty, and she got her just desserts the second I was escorted into the room with four of Windsor Prep's finest. I looked for Birdie while pulled onto the dance floor by Knight, but didn't see her quite yet. I texted her on the way to the dance that I'd be coming, but I'd gotten a different reaction than what I thought I'd get after explaining who I'd be coming with.

*Just be careful,* her text had said, and maybe after all that went on since coming here, that made sense. These Court boys, Royal in particular, had a reputation around this place. She wanted me to watch my back, and I got that. Tonight, the boys seemed to have mine, all of them, even Knight, who hadn't seemed to really care for me in the past. He kept silent during our dances while the other guys mingled on the floor around us, but there was something different about our previous interactions. He was there *with me* tonight instead of against me, and I got that from all the boys. LJ was really fun, albeit a little stiff. Dancing obviously wasn't his forte, but Jax let loose like I'd expect only him to. All five of us did the group dance thing for the most part, the fast dances easy to do that with. We may have gone together, but we were all just here as friends, laughing and having a good time, and it was that way with all the dances with the guys.

At least all but one, of course.

Dances with Royal were different, his hands on my waist and his attention on me different. He was the one I wasn't sure I was here with as friends, but I didn't ask. I just enjoyed the moment, and he did too. He'd been asked to dance by several girls tonight, and even if he wasn't in a dance with me, he turned them down. He waited for me.

"You know Paige and the rest of us always went to dances like this," he said, pulling me close. "All of us hanging out, just being cool. It was easy."

I held him close too, enjoying the way his hard body hit and warmed mine. He, my sister, and the others may have gone to dances together, but I was sure they weren't *quite* like this. They didn't feel like this, heaven. I think I was started to fall for this boy, hard, and that kind of scared me a little.

"You missed school," I mentioned in passing, and he nodded, holding my hand. "You okay?"

"Just need some time," he said. "But that's all over now. I'm here."

I didn't know what was over now, but in any sense, I saw Birdie. She came through the gym doors, she and the other basketball girls laughing, and I had a feeling they might have taken a little smoke break. I caught their attention while with Royal, raising my hand, and though Kiki, Shakira, and the others on the team waved back, I just got a tight smile from Birdie. She really wasn't on the same page as me tonight, but that was okay. I did get it.

"Jax said I was the first girl ever in Windsor House," I said, transferring my attention back to Royal. "Paige never went…"

"Paige never wanted to," he explained his eyes flickering away. "When it came to the Court, that was my thing, never hers."

"So why did you let me in?"

"Maybe I shouldn't have," he said, pulling strong arms around me. "But I guess I don't fucking care anymore."

He was going to pull me in really good this boy and almost kissed me had I not noticed Birdie and our friends again. They stood off the dance floor with their phones, their hands over their mouths, and whatever they were looking at caused a stir amongst them. They looked up at me almost immediately, *all* of them, and had I not been distracted by Knight pushing onto the dance floor to Royal and me, I would have gone over.

"You need to see this," Knight said, his phone in his hand. LJ and Jax were behind him, and whatever needed to be seen, they showed Royal first and not me.

Royal took the phone, and it was like the world whispered around me. I noticed everyone had their phones out, everyone on the dance floor looking at something, but I was the only one not in on whatever was going on.

"What is it?" I asked. "What's going on?"

Royal wouldn't let me see at first, and it was LJ to take Knight's phone and give it to me. There was a news story on the screen, an announcer talking about a local girl who was found downstate. She'd been dragged there... found under a train.

A picture flashed of the girl, only one, but it was enough to make my world around me spin on its axis. I collapsed in arms, boys rushing around me. They spoke words to me, so many words, but I heard none of it.

I needed to throw up.

I ran, ran away from everyone, and I barely made it outside the school before I was on my knees in dirt. I ruined my sister's pretty dress, heaving my guts out as I attempted to forgot what I just saw on a phone screen. My sister, Paige, would never get to wear this dress.

My sister was dead.

*Thank you so much for checking out They The Pretty Stars! Did you know there's an entire website dedicated to the Court High Books with exclusive content, teasers to the next book, Illusions That May, and all other kinds of great freebies??? No? Well, what are you waiting for! Subscribe to my newsletter below and you'll not only get a link to all the yummies listed above but also hear from me about all my new releases and projects. =^)*

My newsletter and link to freebies:

https://bit.ly/2TBbygm

Printed in Great Britain
by Amazon